OPPOSING VIEWPOINTS® SERIES

Police Reform

Other Books of Related Interest

Opposing Viewpoints Series

Mass Incarceration
The Prison Industrial Complex
Racial Discrimination and Criminal Justice

At Issue Series

Policing in America
Public Outrage and Protest
Wrongful Conviction and Exoneration

Current Controversies Series

Homelessness and Street Crime
Immigration, Asylum, and Sanctuary Cities
Police Training and Excessive Force

> "Congress shall make no law … abridging the freedom of speech, or of the press."
>
> *First Amendment to the U.S. Constitution*

The basic foundation of our democracy is the First Amendment guarantee of freedom of expression. The Opposing Viewpoints series is dedicated to the concept of this basic freedom and the idea that it is more important to practice it than to enshrine it.

OPPOSING VIEWPOINTS® SERIES

Police Reform

Eamon Doyle, Book Editor

GREENHAVEN PUBLISHING

Published in 2023 by Greenhaven Publishing, LLC
2544 Clinton Street,
Buffalo NY 14224

First Edition

Articles in Greenhaven Publishing anthologies are often edited for length to meet page requirements. In addition, original titles of these works are changed to clearly present the main thesis and to explicitly indicate the author's opinion. Every effort is made to ensure that Greenhaven Publishing accurately reflects the original intent of the authors. Every effort has been made to trace the owners of the copyrighted material.

Cover image: Daniel Tadevosyan/Shutterstock.com

Library of Congress CataloginginPublication Data

Names: Doyle, Eamon, 1988- editor.
Title: Police reform / Eamon Doyle.
Description: First edition. | New York : Greenhaven Publishing, 2023. | Series: Opposing viewpoints | Includes bibliographical references and index. | Audience: Ages 15+ | Audience: Grades 10-12 | Summary: "Anthology of licensed articles and introductory text and resource material exploring the issue of police reform"-- Provided by publisher.
Identifiers: LCCN 2022024787 | ISBN 9781534509108 (library binding) | ISBN 9781534509092 (paperback)
Subjects: LCSH: Police--United States--Juvenile literature. | Law enforcement--United States--Juvenile literature. | Police brutality--United States--Juvenile literature. | Criminal justice, Administration of--United States--Juvenile literature.
Classification: LCC HV8139 .P648 2023 | DDC 363.20973--dc23/eng/20220610
LC record available at https://lccn.loc.gov/2022024787

Manufactured in the United States of America

Website: http://greenhavenpublishing.com

Contents

Chapter 3: Should the U.S. Ban Qualified Immunity for Law Enforcement Officers?

Chapter 4: Is "Defund the Police" an Effective Strategy for Police Reform?

The Importance of Opposing Viewpoints

Perhaps every generation experiences a period in time in which the populace seems especially polarized, starkly divided on the important issues of the day and gravitating toward the far ends of the political spectrum and away from a consensus-facilitating middle ground. The world that today's students are growing up in and that they will soon enter into as active and engaged citizens is deeply fragmented in just this way. Issues relating to terrorism, immigration, women's rights, minority rights, race relations, health care, taxation, wealth and poverty, the environment, policing, military intervention, the proper role of government—in some ways, perennial issues that are freshly and uniquely urgent and vital with each new generation—are currently roiling the world.

If we are to foster a knowledgeable, responsible, active, and engaged citizenry among today's youth, we must provide them with the intellectual, interpretive, and critical-thinking tools and experience necessary to make sense of the world around them and of the all-important debates and arguments that inform it. After all, the outcome of these debates will in large measure determine the future course, prospects, and outcomes of the world and its peoples, particularly its youth. If they are to become successful members of society and productive and informed citizens, students need to learn how to evaluate the strengths and weaknesses of someone else's arguments, how to sift fact from opinion and fallacy, and how to test the relative merits and validity of their own opinions against the known facts and the best possible available information. The landmark series Opposing Viewpoints has been providing students with just such critical-thinking skills and exposure to the debates surrounding society's most urgent contemporary issues for many years, and it continues to serve this essential role with undiminished commitment, care, and rigor.

The key to the series's success in achieving its goal of sharpening students' critical-thinking and analytic skills resides in its title—

Opposing Viewpoints. In every intriguing, compelling, and engaging volume of this series, readers are presented with the widest possible spectrum of distinct viewpoints, expert opinions, and informed argumentation and commentary, supplied by some of today's leading academics, thinkers, analysts, politicians, policy makers, economists, activists, change agents, and advocates. Every opinion and argument anthologized here is presented objectively and accorded respect. There is no editorializing in any introductory text or in the arrangement and order of the pieces. No piece is included as a "straw man," an easy ideological target for cheap point-scoring. As wide and inclusive a range of viewpoints as possible is offered, with no privileging of one particular political ideology or cultural perspective over another. It's left to each individual reader to evaluate the relative merits of each argument—as he or she sees it, and with the use of ever-growing critical-thinking skills—and grapple with his or her own assumptions, beliefs, and perspectives to determine how convincing or successful any given argument is and how the reader's own stance on the issue may be modified or altered in response to it.

This process is facilitated and supported by volume, chapter, and selection introductions that provide readers with the essential context they need to begin engaging with the spotlighted issues, with the debates surrounding them, and with their own perhaps shifting or nascent opinions on them. In addition, guided reading and discussion questions encourage readers to determine the authors' point of view and purpose, interrogate and analyze the various arguments and their rhetoric and structure, evaluate the arguments' strengths and weaknesses, test their claims against available facts and evidence, judge the validity of the reasoning, and bring into clearer, sharper focus the reader's own beliefs and conclusions and how they may differ from or align with those in the collection or those of their classmates.

Research has shown that reading comprehension skills improve dramatically when students are provided with compelling, intriguing, and relevant "discussable" texts. The subject matter of these collections could not be more compelling, intriguing, or urgently relevant to today's students and the world they are poised to inherit. The anthologized articles and the reading and discussion questions that are included with them also provide the basis for stimulating, lively, and passionate classroom debates. Students who are compelled to anticipate objections to their own argument and identify the flaws in those of an opponent read more carefully, think more critically, and steep themselves in relevant context, facts, and information more thoroughly. In short, using discussable text of the kind provided by every single volume in the Opposing Viewpoints series encourages close reading, facilitates reading comprehension, fosters research, strengthens critical thinking, and greatly enlivens and energizes classroom discussion and participation. The entire learning process is deepened, extended, and strengthened.

For all of these reasons, Opposing Viewpoints continues to be exactly the right resource at exactly the right time—when we most need to provide readers with the critical-thinking tools and skills that will not only serve them well in school but also in their careers and their daily lives as decision-making family members, community members, and citizens. This series encourages respectful engagement with and analysis of opposing viewpoints and fosters a resulting increase in the strength and rigor of one's own opinions and stances. As such, it helps make readers "future ready," and that readiness will pay rich dividends for the readers themselves, for the citizenry, for our society, and for the world at large.

Introduction

> *"Policing is the application of the state's coercive power to produce public safety. We should want as little application of that power as we can possibly have. Public safety should be produced as much as possible by healthy communities."*

—David M. Kennedy, "State Violence, Legitimacy, and the Path to True Public Safety"[1]

The political and social issues surrounding the question of police reform in the United States have a long, complicated history. Throughout U.S. history, policy debates about the role of law enforcement, police procedure, and criminal justice have been closely intertwined with discussions about racism and economic inequality. For instance, many historians trace the origins of the modern American police force to slave patrols in the pre-Civil War era. During periods of political unrest over racial issues (e.g. the civil rights era in the 1960s, the L.A. riots following the Rodney King verdict in 1992), police forces often reacted violently to protest demonstrations. And the U.S. criminal justice system is perceived by large portions of the public to be biased against African Americans and other racial minorities.

Over the course of the 2010s, the widespread use of social media and smartphones with video recording capabilities led to a profusion of new evidence of police brutality, particularly toward young black men. The increased visibility of police violence led to anger and calls for reform. The contemporary protest groups Black Lives Matter and Defund the Police emerged in this era.

But the landscape of police reform in contemporary American society extends beyond the racial issues that surround law enforcement in America. Many critics have described a "militarization" of police forces in America since the late twentieth century—including more powerful weapons, military-style gear, and what some observers have described as a "warrior" mentality. The writer Seth Stoughton elaborates on the latter:

> Under this warrior worldview, officers are locked in intermittent and unpredictable combat with unknown but highly lethal enemies. As a result, officers learn to be afraid. That isn't the word used in law enforcement circles, of course. Vigilant, attentive, cautious, alert, or observant are the terms that appear most often in police publications. But make no mistake, officers don't learn to be vigilant, attentive, cautious, alert, and observant just because it's fun. They do so because they are afraid. Fear is ubiquitous in law enforcement.[2]

Many of the most energetic critics of law enforcement in America cite the "warrior" mentality as among their central concerns when describing the shortcomings of America's police-oriented approach to public safety.

Some proponents of police reform have offered alternative models of public safety, where the scope of police work would be scaled back and replaced in various ways by social workers, mental health professionals, and neighborhood-based community safety organizations. This theory has a close association with the contemporary "Defund the Police" movement, which emerged in the aftermath of George Floyd's murder by a police officer in 2020. The writers Howard Henderson and Ben Yisrael describe the basic idea in the following passage:

> No matter what we choose to call it, defund the police, a reallocation of funding, or a total reimagination, research supports a public health approach to policing. If we are effective, funding public health approaches will reduce the reliance on

> law-and-order policing, save lives and reverse the longstanding slide in the wrong direction. Police must be the last resort, used only when necessary to protect the public from harm. Until then, municipalities will need to prepare for the impact of increased police accountability and transparency. Ultimately the rising costs associated with police misconduct will force police reform, a cost that would have been much cheaper had we listened to those groups most impacted by aggressive policing. To see real change in our society, policymakers must remove the barriers and fund necessary programming.[3]

But there are also plenty of voices, particularly from the conservative side of the political spectrum, speaking out against such reform proposals and defending police work as it currently exists and operates in American society.

Opposing Viewpoints: Police Reform illustrates that the idea of reforming our longstanding policing structure is a complex issue with a number of different dimensions, including legal, political, moral, and practical. In chapters titled "How Widespread Is Police Brutality?"; "Is America's Criminal Justice System Racist?"; "Should the U.S. Ban Qualified Immunity for Law Enforcement Officers?"; and "Is 'Defund the Police' an Effective Strategy for Police Reform?", a variety of voices from different landscapes provide a satisfying overview of law enforcement reform issues in American society today.

Notes

1. David M. Kennedy, "State Violence, Legitimacy, and the Path to True Public Safety," Niskanen Center, July 8, 2020.
2. Seth Stoughton, "Law Enforcement's 'Warrior' Problem," Harvard Law Review, April 10, 2015.
3. Howard Henderson and Ben Yisrael, "7 myths About 'Defunding the Police' Debunked," The Brookings Institution, May 19, 2021.

OPPOSING VIEWPOINTS® SERIES

Chapter 1

How Widespread Is Police Brutality?

Chapter Preface

In many cases, what gives debates about police reform a sense of urgency and fuels both pro-reform and pro-police anger is violence. Throughout recent history, police reform advocates point to specific instances of police brutality, such as the Rodney King beating and the murders of George Floyd and Eric Garner, to demonstrate that an overhaul of the law enforcement system in America is a matter of life and death. Police advocates tend to offer the reverse argument—emphasizing the experiences endured by victims of violent crime and portraying the police as the only thing standing between contemporary American society and a state of full-blown violent anarchy.

If we focus on the details, however, there is a more subtle and complex conversation to be held about the use of force by law enforcement officers, and how police integrate with the communities they are charged with serving. Many reform advocates imagine a scenario where police work could be largely replaced by something closer to social work: strengthening communities, improving the landscape of educational and economic opportunities, etc. Some have referred to this concept in terms of a public health-oriented approach to law enforcement. And in fact, some police officers and law enforcement advocates have expressed interest in limiting the scope of police work to focus more specifically on violent crime and less on duties like traffic enforcement, minor drug violations, and other areas where various social services might be more appropriate—and more effective.

More controversial is the argument advanced by many reform advocates that law enforcement culture is oriented around a "warrior" mentality that encourages police to think of the public in terms of enemies and the possibility of encountering life-threatening dangers in the course of their work. Police advocates tend to respond to this line of argument by pointing out that contemporary American society is extremely violent and that carrying out law enforcement work in that kind of environment can require something like a soldier mentality. These and other oppositional points of view add to the complexities of the debate over police violence and reform.

Viewpoint 1

> *"The evidence from the scholarly literature suggests that the more legitimate the law and the police are in the eyes of America's communities, the less we will actually have to use them."*

Police Violence Is State Violence

David M. Kennedy

In the following excerpted viewpoint David M. Kennedy argues that police brutality should not be tolerated in any way, yet since there rarely seem to be any repercussions, it continues. Kennedy maintains that the state—via policing—has been committing violence against Black Americans and failing to protect throughout throughout history. David M. Kennedy is a professor of criminal justice at John Jay College of Criminal Justice in New York City and the director of the National Network for Safe Communities at John Jay.

"State Violence, Legitimacy, and the Path to True Public Safety," by David M. Kennedy, Niskanen Center, July 8, 2020, https://www.niskanencenter.org/state-violence-legitimacy-and-the-path-to-true-public-safety/.

As you read, consider the following questions:

1. Why is it important for the author to connect police departments with the government or state?
2. What does the author intend by mentioning his professional experience?
3. Why does this viewpoint regard protest movements as opportunities rather than threats?

Let's be clear about what's been happening in the country these last few weeks. Policing is an arm of the state. Police departments and police officers operate under the color of law and as agents of the state, with authority granted by their nation's citizens. That gives their actions special meaning. George Floyd was—literally—killed by his government. Over and over again in America, Black people have been killed, beaten, and otherwise abused by their government through its agents: the police. In the modern era, Rodney King was beaten by his government. Michael Brown was shot and killed by his government. Walter Scott was shot in the back and killed by his government; his government then falsified the shooting scene and lied about what had happened.

This has always been an outrage. But the last several weeks in America have been transformative for how the nation thinks about and responds to police violence. A short time ago—before a Minneapolis police officer killed George Floyd—it would have been unimaginable that hundreds of thousands of both Black and White protesters would take over cities for weeks, advocating for Black lives and protesting police brutality. It would have been unimaginable that those protests would be supported across the political spectrum, that the city council of a major American city would commit to the outright elimination of its police department, and that "defunding" policing would become a live option in the national political discourse—with commitments from the mayors of New York City and Los Angeles. It would have been unimaginable that over a thousand professional athletes would call for an end to the doctrine of "qualified immunity" that protects police violence, that NASCAR would ban the Confederate flag, and that PepsiCo would retire Aunt Jemima.

As somebody who has spent the last three decades working with the police to reduce violent crime, I believe that all of this is for good. I've been part of developing a violence prevention strategy that has a central role for police in partnership with the community and service providers. It can cut homicides—mostly of young Black men—in half or more. It was the source of the so-called "Boston Miracle" over 20 years ago that reduced young people's murders by almost two-thirds. It's the same body of work that has made Oakland, California, a shining star in violence prevention, with homicide and gun violence down by half over the last eight years. I've worked with police to shut down street drug markets in ways that keep dealers out of jail, and to prevent domestic violence victims from being killed without making them bear the risk of prosecuting their abusers or the burden of going underground to hide. I have worked arm in arm with police officers who are courageous, creative, and committed to their communities. In short, I know how much good the right kind of policing can do. But I also know how much damage the wrong kind of policing does—and I support sweeping changes to mend that damage.

In the protests of these last weeks, the government has beaten citizens, driven vehicles into protesters, and fired pepper rounds at journalists. Yes, in those same protests, police officers have been shot, police stations burned, and businesses looted. But police violence is fundamentally different from private violence. It is in no way to diminish the wrongness of crimes committed by the public to say: we know that people will do these things—kill, rape, and rob. It is because we know that people will do these things that in democracies there is the social contract: a state monopoly on violence and coercion, which speaks through the law and makes that law operative through institutions, including the police. If a protestor punches you in the face, he has committed a crime. The social contract says that it is wrong, and the state has the power to stop it. If a police officer punches you in the face, you have been assaulted by your government. It is simply a statement of the human condition to say: people will forever and always kill each other, no matter how hard we try to prevent it. If we say: our government will forever and always kill us, and beat us, and do us violence under the color of law, no matter how hard we try to prevent it, that is fundamentally different. That is an admission and an acceptance of the failure of the state of our democracy, and the American experiment.

Yet, for all of American history, the government has done exactly that to Black Americans. Slavery was violence. Reinstituting slavery after Reconstruction through the criminal justice system and convict leasing was violence. Lynching was violence. Setting dogs and fire hoses on the civil rights movement was violence. As was the FBI trying to drive Martin Luther King Jr. to suicide was violence, and the city of Philadelphia bombing and burning a city block. Zero-tolerance policing, rampant stop-and-frisk, the disparity in crack and powder cocaine sentencing, and mass incarceration were and are the racialized use of the state's coercive power.

Where the government has not done violence to Black people, it has failed to protect them. The homicide rate for Black men ages 18-34 is almost 18 times that of White men the same age. Homicides of Black men and women go unsolved. White men in military garb carrying rifles gather safely at statehouses; Black men going running are hunted down, shot, and killed. Black people fear their government. They have "the talk" with their kids and worry when they go to school and drive their cars. They are unsafe walking, shopping, swimming, sleeping at Yale. They know what asking a White woman to leash her dog can mean. Black police officers, often required to carry their weapons off-duty, fear being killed by their fellow officers.

This is what so misses the point when people who don't get it say, "But most Black homicide victims are not killed by police." Most White people are not killed in terrorist attacks; 9/11 and everything like it represents a tiny fraction of the White body count over the last decades. But the United States government completely reoriented national security after 9/11; we're still at war. Most White kids are not killed in mass shootings, but the country is pouring resources into school safety. Terror and mass shootings cut to the core of what it means to live one's life, feel safe and secure, and trust that one's family and loved ones will be safe and secure. And when the mass of White people feels threatened by terror and mass shootings, their country leaps to their defense. Being Black in America has meant knowing that one's family and loved ones are never safe and secure because your country can hurt you and them at any moment. It has meant being subject to state violence and to the state's protection of private violence, in a nation forged out of, structured by, and soaked in racism. Black Americans have always known that. White Americans are apparently starting to get it. What is going on now in the nation is a rejection of that arc of history.

The protest movement represents core American values and deserves broad bipartisan support. It is no threat to our efforts to prevent crime and violence; indeed, it represents an opportunity to make those efforts much more successful. That is because it can support the emergence of a fundamentally better way to produce public safety. The evidence from the scholarly literature suggests that the more legitimate the law and the police are in the eyes of America's communities, the less we will actually have to use them. And while "law and order" has traditionally been a platform for the political right, this goal—using the state's coercive power no more than absolutely necessary—is one that conservatives should find easy to embrace. In a very real way, more legitimacy in the realm of policing means less government.

[...]

Viewpoint 2

> *"It is the armed representatives of the capitalist state … against the most impoverished sections of the working class."*

Police Violence Is Focused Overwhelmingly on Men Lowest on the Socioeconomic Ladder

Benjamin Mateus

In the following viewpoint, Benjamin Mateus challenges the notion that police violence targets Black and Brown citizens to a systematically disproportionate degree, pointing to several misleading statistics that academics and journalists have used to promote the concept of race-based police violence. He also introduces data on other demographic categories related to socioeconomic class, geography, and population density to show that rates of police violence and disparities in the victim demographics respond to a complex mix of social dynamics, and that among these dynamics race is ultimately less significant than social class. Dr. Benjamin Mateus is a physician and a journalist who writes regularly for the World Socialist Web Site (WSWS).

"Behind the Epidemic of Police Killings in America: Class, Poverty and Race," by Benjamin Mateus, World Socialist Web Site, December 20, 2018. Reprinted by permission.

As you read, consider the following questions:

1. According to the author, why are some of the publicly reported statistics on race and police violence misleading?
2. Why are geography and population density (i.e. urban vs. rural areas) important to consider when analyzing statistics on police violence?
3. Why does the author believe that race is an "unscientific" demographic category?

The steady rise in police killings in the United States is the manifestation of an ongoing civil war between the ruling elite, the top one-tenth of one percent, and the working class. It is not "white cops vs. black youth," as portrayed by the media and groups like Black Lives Matter and the pseudo-left, anxious to elevate race over class. It is the armed representatives of the capitalist state (frequently black and Hispanic, as well as white) against the most impoverished sections of the working class, white, black, Hispanic and Native American.

This study reviews all the data available on police shootings for the year 2017, and analyzes it based on geography, income, and poverty levels, as well as race. It identifies a major omission in all the published accounts: the vast and rising death toll among working-class white men in rural and small-town America, who are being killed by police at rates that approach those of black men in urban areas.

Police violence is focused overwhelmingly on men lowest on the socio-economic ladder: in rural areas outside the South, predominately white men; in the Southwest, disproportionately Hispanic men; in mid-size and major cities, disproportionately black men. Significantly, in the rural South, where the population is racially mixed, white men and black men are killed by police at nearly identical rates. What unites these victims of police violence is not their race, but their class status (as well as, of course, their gender).

The wave of killings by police officers that occurred in the period from 2014 to 2016, many caught on personal smartphones and released through social media channels, led to an outpouring of popular rage against these crimes. Protests against these horrific killings perpetrated by the police officers, who for the most part face little or no consequences, have become commonplace. Some of the best-known cases include:

- Eric Garner, July 17, 2014, Staten Island, NY (Grand jury did not indict Officer Pantaleo.)
- Michael Brown, age 18, August 9, 2014, Ferguson, MO (Grand jury did not indict Officer Wilson.)
- Laquan McDonald, October 20, 2014, Chicago, IL (Officer Van Dyke convicted of second-degree murder. On December 14, 2018, Van Dyke was denied a new trial, with sentencing set for January 18, 2019.)
- Tamir Rice, age 12, November 23, 2014, Cleveland, OH (Wrongful death suit settled. No charges brought against the officers.)
- Walter Scott, April 4, 2015, North Charleston, SC (Because of a bystander's video, Officer Slager was convicted of second-degree murder and sentenced to 20 years.)
- Freddie Gray, April 12, 2015, Baltimore, MD (He died of spinal cord injuries during a "rough ride" in the back of a police van. Six officers were indicted but two were acquitted, a third ended in a hung jury, after which charges were dropped against the others.)
- Sandra Bland, July 10, 2015, Prairie View, TX (Found dead in her cell and ruled a suicide. The arresting officer was fired and indicted for perjury. No one charged with her death.)
- Alton Sterling, July 5, 2016, Baton Rouge, LA (District attorney decided not to bring charges against two policemen.)
- Philando Castile, July 6, 2016, Falcon Heights, MN (Officer Yanez acquitted of all charges a year later, then fired.)

All of these victims were black and poor. All the killings took place in urban areas or their suburbs. In all but the Castile case, the officers involved were white. These demographic characteristics were well publicized and became the media template for all such police killings. But a more thorough investigation shows that the killing of poor blacks by white cops is only one aspect of the reign of terror by American police against the working class, and not even the most common form of such killings.

Enormous resources have been mobilized to spread the "race, not class" mythology of police killings. Black Lives Matter (BLM) was formed in the aftermath of Trayvon Martin's killing by neighborhood watchman George Zimmerman in 2012. As a response to the growing tension within these communities associated with these killings, BLM was used to channel the anger along racialist lines and, ultimately and politically, in support of the Democratic Party.

As we wrote in 2017, "From the beginning, the 'mothers of the movement' Alicia Garza, Patrisse Cullors and Opal Tometi—who collectively adopted the famous hashtag—specifically opposed uniting blacks, whites and immigrants against the brutal class-war policies of the capitalist state. Instead, the group did its best to confine anti-police violence protests within the framework of the capitalist system and push a racialist and pro-capitalist agenda."

Big money donors lined up behind BLM. The Ford Foundation made a six-year $100 million investment in the organization. BLM garnered endorsements from companies such as Facebook, Nike and Spotify. BLM has gone on to partner with Fortune 500 New York ad agency J. Walter Thompson (JWT) to create "the biggest and most easily accessible black business database in the country."

The Data on Police Killings

Before 2015, two federal databases, from the FBI and Bureau of Justice Statistics (BJS), were the main sources used to track police shootings. However, these figures, self-reported by the police, have been found to be incomplete and inaccurate. Accordingly, several private groups and media outlets began to systematically track police killings through news reports, publishing the data on their websites.

The Washington Post tracks people "shot dead" by police, while the Guardian records "all people killed by police, regardless of the means" and Fatal Encounters attempts to count all police killings as far back as the year 2000. Fatal Encounters, besides using news sources, also uses several other public databases and research methods. In 2015, the Washington Post counted 990 shot dead while the Guardian counted 1,146 killed. Fatal Encounters counted 1,357 killed.

Academicians and researchers, to provide a veneer of scientific corroboration to the racialist perspective promulgated by mainstream media, have been using the information in these databases to publish peer-reviewed articles to substantiate their perspective on identity politics, push through racialist agendas, and direct the national discussion on these issues. However, there is little substance to their analytical approach, which generally avoids the socio-economic dimension to the phenomenon of police killings, or at best, treats it as one more (usually lesser) factor, in the name of "intersectionality," in which class is blended in to the basic framework of identity politics.

By example, a recently published paper in the American Journal of Public Health titled, "Risk of Police-Involved Death by Race/Ethnicity and Place, United States, 2012–2018," toes the line that "race plays a powerful role in explanations of police-involved killings in the United States." Their results note that in the US police kill on average 2.8 people per day. Blacks are killed at 1.9 to 2.4 deaths per 100,000 per year, a threefold higher rate than whites, who are killed by police at a rate of 0.6 to 0.7 per 100,000. Beyond these rudimentary statistics there is little else to take from the study than to accept the authors' conclusions unquestioningly, "Indeed, our results show that—like other police-related outcomes, which vary across the nation according to local political and social forces—police-involved deaths are contingent upon local contextual environments. Structural racism, racialized criminal-legal systems, anti-immigrant mobilizations, and racial politics all likely play a role in explaining where police killings are most frequent and who is most likely to be a victim."

Race Is a Significant Factor

African-Americans are at greater risk of being killed by police, even though they are less likely to pose an objective threat to law enforcement, according to new data-driven research by Northeastern professor Matt Miller. [...]

"One in 15 firearm deaths is at the hands of police; among African-Americans it's about one in 10," says Miller, a professor of health sciences and epidemiology who has been researching injury and violence prevention for two decades. "Which isn't to say that these shootings are all unjustified. But it sure makes you feel like we should try really hard to figure out how to use less lethal ways of arresting someone's threatening behavior."

Instead of approaching the study with a point of view to be proved or disproved, the researchers set out on a fact-finding mission. They spent two years analyzing the two-year database of 603 firearm homicides by police. They tagged and coded the narratives to put each shooting into context, and then ran the detailed results through a computer program.

"The computer looked at the variations in the data and grouped the victims into categories," says Miller. "It turned out that there were seven categories that fit the statistics."

The seven subtypes of police shootings set apart victims who were armed (with guns or knives) or unarmed, victims who were violent or non-violent, and other crucial details. Among those who were unarmed and appeared to show no objective threat to police, nearly two-thirds of the victims were Hispanic or Black.

Miller noted that none of the seven categories accounted for "suicide by cop," in which victims seek to end their own lives by willfully provoking a police shooting. Instead, suicidal people were distributed across all seven categories.

In every subtype, African-Americans were victims at a rate higher than their proportion to the national population. "This disparity is at its most extreme among incidents involving unarmed victims who pose no apparent threat to law enforcement," says Joey Wertz, a medical student at the University of California Los Angeles who was first author of the study.

"1,000 people in the US Die Every Year in Police Shootings. Who Are They?" by Ian Thomsen, Northeastern University, April 16, 2020.

The Method of This Study

The present study was undertaken to better understand the demographics and economic aspects of police killings in the US, treating police killings as though we were observing an epidemic and seeking to understand the main risk factors that made sections of the population more or less vulnerable. We used the 2017 data from the Washington Post database for our analysis. These were cross-referenced with the KilledbyPolice.net website to ensure accuracy and attempt to fill in missing information such as race, name, and age of some of the victims.

News reports from approximately 15 to 20 percent of these events were reviewed to glean the context of some of these killings as well as help locate the site of shooting for further in-depth analysis. We used information on the location of the shooting to perform a ZIP Code analysis for some of the metropolitan centers and medium-sized cities where blacks were killed at a much higher proportion than in the population. The US Census Bureau website was used to obtain demographic and economic data on states, cities and towns where police killings took place. Data USA and City-Data.com websites were used for population centers under 5,000 people. Economic data used included Median Household Incomes (MHI), Percentage in Poverty (PP), and employment and "not in the workforce" categories to determine the role of these factors in police killings.

Academic studies and news reports use national demographics to compare the rate of those killed by their race. For instance, blacks make up approximately 12 percent of the US population, but they make up about 25 percent of those killed by police. Therefore, blacks are killed by police at more than twice their representation. These numbers are standardized to a rate of numbers killed per 100,000 to form a consistent unit to compare across racial groups.

It should be understood that we had to use the category of "race" despite its completely unscientific character, because virtually all data on police killings describes the victims in such terms. More than three percent of the adult US population, and ten percent of all children, are officially categorized as "mixed race," and from a historical standpoint, the proportion of Americans whose ancestry combines white, black and Native American is even larger. But victims of police killings, and their killers, are not usually categorized in media or government reports in that fashion.

Our statistics also used this methodology to conform to the published literature. However, our hypothesis differs from the published studies. The United States is not homogenously diverse. There are significant variations from state to state and from population centers like metropolises to small rural communities in how the demographics are configured. The Southeast states have large black populations in both urban and rural areas, the Midwest is predominately white, particularly outside city centers, and the Southwest has a very high Hispanic population. Metropolitan centers have higher minority populations while rural communities have a preponderance of white people. There are also considerable socioeconomic variations within these regions.

We tabulated the population estimates and demographics based on the locations where police killings took place which allowed us to compare these regions against the nation as a whole. This also provided the ability to compare economic data for these regions and provide a more accurate estimate of the real picture.

We used the Excel spreadsheet for performing and tabulating the basic statistics. The entire Washington Post data set was imported for this analysis. Web-based chi-squared tests were performed using analytic software to estimate confidence intervals and determine the significance of the findings, a statistical method used to denote a difference that has a low probability of being a chance occurrence. The P-value of 0.05 or less connotes that there is less than a 5 percent probability that the significance in the finding was due to chance. A P-value closer to 1.00 suggests that differences are random or minor. We also employed statistics that looked at observed vs. expected outcomes in each state. The observed outcomes are the reported racial distribution of killings in each state. The expected numbers are derived from the states' actual demographics.

For example, in the state of Alabama, there were 25 people killed. Fourteen (56 percent) were identified as white, seven (28 percent) were black, and 1 (4 percent) was Hispanic. The actual state demographics are 65.8 percent white, 26.8 percent black and 4.2 percent Hispanic. The observed vs. expected outcomes P-value was 0.892 for blacks, meaning that the racial difference was not significant. This has enormous political importance: in Alabama, a state which historically is a byword for racially motivated police violence, there was no "preference" by the police for blacks as targets over whites. Similar "neutrality" by the police was found in Mississippi, an equally backward state from the standpoint of its history of racism. The racial explanation of police violence falls apart in precisely the locations where it should be most blatant.

Viewpoint 3

> *"[I]n order for administrative policies to change officer behavior, the policy must clearly dictate what officers can and cannot do, must be widely communicated, and must be enforced."*

Analyzing Use-of-Force Statistics Is Difficult and Complex

Candice Norwood

In the following viewpoint Candice Norwood analyzes the landscape of quantitative research on the use of force by law enforcement agencies in the United States. She highlights the complexity of reviewing most publicly available, nationwide statistics, which is largely due to the fact that police departments and other law enforcement agencies are subject to different requirements in terms of how they document and report use-of-force cases. She also looks at whether different reporting requirements can reduce overall use-of-force numbers, and which requirements tend to be most effective. Candice Norwood is a journalist and researcher for the nonprofit publication The 19th. Previously she was a reporter with PBS NewsHour, Governing Magazine, and Bloomberg News.

"Can Use of Force Restrictions Change Police Behavior? Here's What We Know" by Candice Norwood, PBS NewsHour, July 23, 2020. Reprinted by permission.

As you read, consider the following questions:

1. What are some of the differences in how law enforcement agencies are required to report use-of-force statistics from jurisdiction to jurisdiction and from state to state?
2. Which reporting requirements are most effective in reducing overall use-of-force numbers?
3. How can changes in law enforcement administrative policies result in real changes in how officers interact with suspects and the public?

The phrase "I can't breathe"—used by both Eric Garner and George Floyd in their fatal encounters with police—has become a rallying cry for a nationwide movement demanding an end to excessive use of force by police.

In the wake of Floyd's death, there has been a renewed call from reform advocates to restrict police use of force. But measuring the impact of different restrictions can be complicated, making it hard to get a clear picture of whether they are effective. Some officers have also expressed concern that significant limitations may jeopardize their safety or prevent them from doing their jobs effectively.

Some cities are proposing additional regulations to their use of force policies. Others are implementing trainings on bias or de-escalation. President Donald Trump issued an executive order on policing last month that calls for a federal database to track incidents of excessive use of force. Two pieces of legislation introduced in Congress, also in June—one by House Democrats and another by Senate Republicans—sought to limit chokeholds and encourage different training and alternatives to force.

Researchers said that what the country knows about how police use force, as well as the success of proposals to reduce it, is limited. What is considered an unnecessary use of force can be different from department to department. Federal and state data tracking use of force is lacking, and the quality of policies and training—what skills or techniques they emphasize—also varies.

Research and Data on Use of Force Is Lacking

The U.S. has more than 12,000 local law enforcement agencies, and none are required to report use of force incidents to the Justice Department.

In recent years, the federal government has made efforts to collect more data on police use of force, but participation is voluntary. The FBI's National Use-of-Force Data Collection project, launched in 2019, received submissions from 40 percent of police. The findings of the information gathered so far have not yet been published.

Most states do not have a standardized system for police departments to report use of force, said Seth Stoughton, an associate professor of law at the University of South Carolina who worked as a police officer in Florida for five years.

"We really don't have any comprehensive data federally or at a state level," Stoughton said, adding that the available federal data is "wildly inaccurate." The most comprehensive tracking of police use of force or fatal encounters do not come from the federal government, he said, but rather from journalists.

In 2015, the Washington Post began tracking fatal shootings by on-duty police officers across the country. Between 2015 and 2020, the Post found more than 5,000 fatal officer-involved shootings. But not every fatal encounter involves a shooting, as exhibited in the cases of Garner and Floyd.

A report from the Guardian found that police killed 1,093 people in 2016, of whom 1,011 died of gunshot wounds. Another comprehensive database, by NJ Advance Media, tracked five years worth of use-of-force reports—72,677 in total—from every local police department in New Jersey. Among the project's findings: Ten percent of police officers accounted for 38 percent of all instances of use of force.

These three investigations do not assess whether force was justified in any of the cases.

Research indicates that of the roughly 60 million police-civilian encounters in the U.S. each year, about 1.8 percent may involve use of force, Stoughton said, but states and departments do not have uniform definitions of "force" and what interactions officers are required to report. Lower level uses of force like a shove or tackle to the ground are more likely to go unreported, Stoughton said.

The variation between police jurisdictions underscores the need for a national database to provide a centralized way to identify and compare trends, said Kami Chavis, a professor and director of the criminal justice program at Wake Forest University School of Law.

Police Are More Likely to Use Force Against People of Color

Researchers who spoke with the NewsHour said disparities exist in how police use force against people from different racial groups, but measuring these differences is complicated. Many studies analyze police killings against nationwide Census data, while some try to account for crime rates in a particular area.

The Washington Post report found that fatal police shooting rates were twice as high among Black Americans as they were among white Americans, and Hispanic Americans had the second highest rate of fatal police encounters. An analysis from The Guardian found that in 2016 police killed Native Americans at the highest rates (10.13 per million people), followed by Black people (6.66 per million). The rate for Latino people was 3.23 per million, and 2.9 per million for white people. The NJ Advance Media investigation concluded that statewide in New Jersey, a Black person was more than three times more likely to face police use of force. And a 2019 national study from university researchers found that Black people are 2.5 times more likely than white people to be killed by police.

One Bureau of Justice Statistics survey determined that in 2015, reported rates of nonfatal threats or uses of force were also higher for Black and Hispanic people—3.3 percent and 3.0 percent, respectively—compared to 1.3 percent for white people.

But it's hard to measure racial disparities, in part because every case has a unique set of circumstances, said Robin Engel, director of the International Association of Chiefs of Police/University of Cincinnati Center for Police Research and Policy. Simply taking the total number of Black people killed by police and comparing it to their overall population size is not a good comparison because it removes the situational factors that may play a role in the use of force, Engel said.

"I'm not claiming that [racial disparities] are not real. They are. It's very clear there are racial and ethnic disparities," Engel said. "But the reasons for those disparities is what we really need to better understand as social scientists so that we can better inform the solutions."

One of the strongest predictors of whether police use force is civilian resistance, she said. Use of force is also more likely when officers are engaged in enforcement activities like making an arrest, Stoughton said. However, these predictors do not speak to different reasons people of color might be more likely to encounter an officer in the first place.

These reasons can include disparate decision making in how police are assigned to different neighborhoods, as well as whether and why people choose to call the police, Stoughton said. Incidents of Black people having the police called on them while sleeping on their university campuses, barbecuing and birdwatching, among other activities, have gained national attention. Numerous high-profile cases of police killings also involve Black people who were unarmed and engaged in nonviolent, low-level offenses.

Some of this behavior can be explained by racial bias, said Jennifer Eberhardt, a Stanford University psychologist and leading researcher on the science of bias. In a series of studies, she found that a group of police officers and a group of graduate students were each more likely to associate Black faces rather than white faces with images and words related to crime, such as knives or guns.

One California police chief told the NewsHour he believes racial disparities can be a problem in policing, but added that officers face a difficult task when making split second decisions about whether to investigate a potential crime or to walk away.

"Ultimately it's about communicating the role the police have and the job of trying to maintain public safety," said John Perez, chief of the Pasadena Police Department and research fellow with the National Police Foundation.

To assist with this goal, Perez's department began working with a nonprofit in 2018 called Why'd You Stop Me, which seeks to foster positive civilian-police interactions by dispelling misconceptions about police to the community and training officers to understand community issues.

Efforts to Regulate and Reduce Use of Force in Policing

Currently, 36 states have laws regulating lethal and non-lethal force, Stoughton and other researchers wrote in a piece for The Atlantic. More than three-quarters of those statutes were adopted in the 1970s, and most have not been amended recently, according to their findings.

For states without statutes, courts have the discretion to interpret use of force cases. Courts often evaluate use of force by referring to the Fourth Amendment, which is meant to regulate seizures, Stoughton said.

In recent years, some police departments and states have moved to limit officers' use of force. One notable example is Cincinnati, which entered into an agreement with the Justice Department in 2002 that mandated sweeping changes to the city's police department, including restrictions on use of force. Engel's research found that between 1999 and 2014, Cincinnati saw a 69 percent decline in police use-of-force incidents, a 56 percent reduction in citizen injuries during police encounters and a 42 percent decrease in citizen complaints

The city of Camden, New Jersey, dissolved and rebuilt its police force in 2014. In 2019, Camden police adopted an 18-page policy that emphasized de-escalation and authorized deadly force only as a last resort.

"It started with two real principles that were laid as the cornerstones for how we would use force. One is that the sanctity of human life underpins everything that we do," Scott Thomson, the city's police chief until 2019, told the PBS NewsHour Weekend's Hari Sreenivasan. "We review every incident of force that's used with multiple layers of review from first line supervisor to the commander, to an internal affair review to the training unit review."

Camden found that civilian excessive force complaints declined by 95 percent from a peak of 65 complaints in 2014 to three complaints in 2019.

After the 2018 police shooting death of Stephon Clark, a 22-year-old Black man, California enacted one of the country's strictest use-of-force laws, which only allows police to use deadly force in the necessary defense of the officer's or another person's life. That same year, Pasadena police chief Perez implemented a 30-day review requirement for all use of force incidents in his department, which he said allows them to more quickly identify and discuss potentially unnecessary use of force incidents. Between 2018 and 2020, Perez said the number of use of force incidents decreased by 50 percent.

Tennessee, Delaware and Iowa also have laws that require officers to exhaust other "reasonable" means before using deadly force. And in the weeks since George Floyd's death, several states and cities have moved to make changes such as banning chokeholds or no-knock warrants, Chavis of Wake Forest said.

"Now is the time for a meaningful change so that no one, especially black men and women, has to ever again think 'that could have been me," Isaiah McKinnon, a retired chief of the Detroit Police Department, wrote in a USA Today piece that recounted his experience being stopped by one of his own officers.

But a policy change is one of many things that may affect officer behavior, and may not change the rate of fatal encounters, Stoughton said. For example, he pointed out that the available data between 2015 and 2018 suggests officers killed more people per capita in Tennessee (about 3.6 per million people) than in Florida (2.9 per million), a state that gives broad authorization for officers to use deadly force.

Evidence indicates that in order for administrative policies to change officer behavior, the policy must clearly dictate what officers can and cannot do, must be widely communicated, and must be enforced, said Michael White, a professor at Arizona State University's School of Criminology and Criminal Justice.

A 2016 report by the Use of Force Project looked at 91 police departments and assessed eight different force-related policies various departments had in place. Among these, the report found the policies most effective at reducing police-involved killings were those that require comprehensive reporting of when officers use force (25 percent reduction), those that require officers to exhaust all other reasonable means before using a firearm (25 percent reduction), and those that ban chokeholds and strangleholds (22 percent reduction).

The report found that police departments that had implemented four or more of the eight policies had 37 percent fewer police-involved killings than those with zero or one policy in place, and that departments with all eight policies in place would kill 72 percent fewer people, on average, between 2015 and 2016.

When it comes to bias or de-escalation training, research on their efficacy is virtually non-existent. Over the last decade police departments have shown a growing interest in both styles of training to mitigate use of force or address racial disparities. As of 2017, 16 states required officers to have de-escalation training, according to American Public Media, eight of which enacted the policies after the 2014 shooting of Michael Brown in Ferguson, Missouri. A CBS News report found that 57 percent of 155 police departments it contacted had implemented racial bias training in the five years since Brown's death.

In January of this year, Engel and other researchers published a systematic review of studies that look at the effectiveness of de-escalation training. "And do you know how many we found for policing? None," Engel said. "Not one study had been conducted to examine the impact of de-escalation training on officer attitudes or behavior."

Of the 64 studies examining de-escalation training for other industries like nursing and psychiatry, Engel said the quality of the methodology was not strong, but the findings showed "slight-to-moderate individual and organizational improvements" as a result of the training. Based on this and anecdotal evidence, "there's reason to be optimistic about de-escalation training," Engel said.

On bias, there's hardly any study on the effectiveness of training, Eberhardt said. Furthermore, she said, evidence indicates that simply becoming aware of a bias does not change behavior.

The composition and quality of the training varies, said Lorie Fridell, CEO of Fair and Impartial Policing, a company that has provided bias training to officers in New York City, Baton Rouge, Louisiana, Arlington, Texas and others. For Eberhardt, the most effective programs look to disrupt circumstances that may trigger bias. Fridell said her focus isn't about eliminating bias but instead "managing bias." Both strategies may involve prompting police to ask certain questions of themselves to figure out why they are engaging a particular civilian.

"Rather than simply informing people about the conditions under which bias is most likely to occur, we should be actually working to change those conditions," Eberhardt said.

Fridell said the attitudes of officers in her company's bias training range "somewhere between defensive and outright hostile." But when she approaches bias as a human and societal problem rather than just a police problem, they become much more receptive, she said.

Bias and de-escalation training has received more broad support from law enforcement and lawmakers, but officers have voiced frustration over use-of-force restrictions and disciplinary action taken against them for using force. In 2019, the Crime and Justice Institute released a report on focus groups conducted with police officers in Baltimore. The summary said "officers fear and believe that too many documented uses of force will be used as evidence against them and result in disciplinary action, a criminal investigation, or restrict reassignment and advancement within the department." It added that the officers said they felt less safe on the job and apprehensive about when to use force.

Perez of the Pasadena Police Department said he respects the Black Lives Matter movement's calls for reform but he also understands some of the anxieties officers may have regarding strict limitations. Rigid policies that don't take into account the challenges of policing could make officers hesitate to take actions to protect themselves during a confrontation, Perez said. "It could go too far," Perez said. "It requires so much more discussion to make the changes that we need. We have to get the empirical evidence and look at it to protect the young officers who are working in the streets."

Advocates, however, continue to push forward with proposals for sweeping systemic changes. As conversations about policing continue, Eberhardt said, it will take more than training or restrictions on excessive use of force, but they are an important start, she said. "It's about addressing the entire context under which these police-civilian interactions occur."

Viewpoint 4

> *"Today, live streaming, tweets and Facebook posts have blasted the incidents of police brutality, beyond the black community and into the mainstream media."*

The U.S. Has a Long, Painful History of Police Brutality

Katie Nodjimbadem

In the following viewpoint Katie Nodjimbaden contextualizes the 2016 shooting death of Philando Castile at the hands of police officers in terms of the history of law enforcement violence against Black and brown citizens throughout American history. The author discusses some of the reasons why the use of force by police officers is directed disproportionately at the Black community and looks at how those reasons are rooted in specific historical events. She also examines how the wide availability of smartphone technologies have impacted the public awareness of police violence and its impact on minority communities. Katie Nodjimbaden is a journalist and Fulbright Fellow based in Abidjan, Côte d'Ivoire.

"The Long, Painful History of Police Brutality in the U.S.," by Katie Nodjimbadem, Smithsonian Magazine, July 27, 2017. Reprinted by permission.

As you read, consider the following questions:

1. Why is the history of policing in America relevant when it comes to analyzing racism in law enforcement today?
2. How have social media and smartphone technologies like live streaming impacted public awareness of police violence?
3. What are some examples of major protests against law enforcement violence in American history?

Last month, hours after a jury acquitted former police officer Jeronimo Yanez of manslaughter in the shooting death of 32-year-old Philando Castile, protesters in St. Paul, Minnesota, shutdown Interstate 94. With signs that read: "Black Lives Matter" and "No Justice, No Peace," the chant of "Philando, Philando" rang out as they marched down the highway in the dark of night.

The scene was familiar. A year earlier, massive protests had erupted when Yanez killed Castile, after pulling him over for a broken taillight. Dashcam footage shows Yanez firing through the open window of Castile's car, seconds after Castile disclosed that he owned and was licensed to carry a concealed weapon.

A respected school nutritionist, Castile was one of 233 African-Americans shot and killed by police in 2016, a startling number when demographics are considered. African-Americans make up 13 percent of the U.S. population but account for 24 percent of people fatally shot by police. According to the Washington Post, blacks are "2.5 times as likely as white Americans to be shot and killed by police officers."

Today's stories are anything but a recent phenomenon. A cardboard placard in the collections of the Smithsonian's National Museum of African American History and Culture and on view in the new exhibition "More Than a Picture," underscores that reality.

The yellowing sign is a reminder of the continuous oppression and violence that has disproportionately shaken black communities for generations—"We Demand an End to Police Brutality Now!" is painted in red and white letters.

"The message after 50 years is still unresolved," remarks Samuel Egerton, a college professor, who donated the poster to the museum. He carried it in protest during the 1963 March on Washington. Five decades later, the poster's message rings alarmingly timely. Were it not for the yellowed edges, the placard could almost be mistaken for a sign from any of the Black Lives Matter marches of the past three years.

"There are those who are asking the devotees of civil rights, 'When will you be satisfied?" said Martin Luther King, Jr. in his iconic "I Have a Dream" speech at the 1963 march. His words continue to resonate today after a long history of violent confrontations between African-American citizens and the police. "We can never be satisfied as long as the Negro is the victim of the unspeakable horrors of police brutality."

"This idea of police brutality was very much on people's minds in 1963, following on the years, decades really, of police abuse of power and then centuries of oppression of African-Americans," says William Pretzer, senior history curator at the museum.

Modern policing did not evolve into an organized institution until the 1830s and '40s when northern cities decided they needed better control over quickly growing populations. The first American police department was established in Boston in 1838. The communities most targeted by harsh tactics were recent European immigrants. But, as African-Americans fled the horrors of the Jim Crow south, they too became the victims of brutal and punitive policing in the northern cities where they sought refuge.

In 1929, the Illinois Association for Criminal Justice published the Illinois Crime Survey. Conducted between 1927 and 1928, the survey sought to analyze causes of high crime rates in Chicago and Cook County, especially among criminals associated with Al Capone. But also the survey provided data on police activity—although African-Americans made up just five percent of the area's population, they constituted 30 percent of the victims of police killings, the survey revealed.

"There was a lot of one-on-one conflict between police and citizens and a lot of it was initiated by the police," says Malcolm D. Holmes, a sociology professor at the University of Wyoming, who has researched and written about the topic of police brutality extensively.

That same year, President Herbert Hoover established the National Commission on Law Observance and Enforcement to investigate crime related to prohibition in addition to policing tactics. Between 1931 and 1932, the commission published the findings of its investigation in 14 volumes, one of which was titled "Report on Lawlessness in Law Enforcement." The realities of police brutality came to light, even though the commission did not address racial disparities outright.

During the Civil Rights Era, though many of the movement's leaders advocated for peaceful protests, the 1960s were fraught with violent and destructive riots.

Aggressive dispersion tactics, such as police dogs and fire hoses, against individuals in peaceful protests and sit-ins were the most widely publicized examples of police brutality in that era. But it was the pervasive violent policing in communities of color that built distrust at a local, everyday level.

One of the deadliest riots occurred in Newark in 1967 after police officers severely beat black cab driver John Smith during a traffic stop. Twenty-six people died and many others were injured during the four days of unrest. In 1968, President Lyndon B. Johnson organized the National Advisory Commission on Civil Disorders to investigate the causes of these major riots.

The origins of the unrest in Newark weren't unique in a police versus citizen incident. The commission concluded "police actions were 'final' incidents before the outbreak of violence in 12 of the 24 surveyed disorders."

The commission identified segregation and poverty as indicators and published recommendations for reducing social inequalities, recommending an "expansion and reorientation of the urban renewal program to give priority to projects directly assisting low-income households to obtain adequate housing." Johnson, however, rejected the commission's recommendations.

Black newspapers reported incidents of police brutality throughout the early and mid-20th century and the popularization of radio storytelling spread those stories even further. In 1991, following the beating of cab driver Rodney King, video footage vividly told the story of police brutality on television to a much wider audience. The police officers, who were acquitted of the crime, had hit King more than 50 times with their batons.

Today, live streaming, tweets and Facebook posts have blasted the incidents of police brutality, beyond the black community and into the mainstream media. Philando Castile's fiancée, Diamond Reynolds, who was in the car with her daughter when he was shot, streamed the immediate aftermath of the shooting on her phone using Facebook live.

"Modern technology allows, indeed insists, that the white community take notice of these kinds of situations and incidents," says Pretzer.

And as technology has evolved, so has the equipment of law enforcement. Police departments with military-grade equipment have become the norm in American cities. Images of police officers in helmets and body armor riding through neighborhoods in tanks accompany stories of protests whenever one of these incidents occurs.

"What we see is a continuation of an unequal relationship that has been exacerbated, made worse if you will, by the militarization and the increase in fire power of police forces around the country," says Pretzer.

The resolution to the problem, according to Pretzer, lies not only in improving these unbalanced police-community relationships, but, more importantly, in eradicating the social inequalities that perpetuate these relationships that sustain distrust and frustration on both sides.

‘There’s a tendency to stereotype people as being more or less dangerous. There’s a reliance upon force that goes beyond what is necessary to accomplish police duty,” says Holmes. “There’s a lot of this embedded in the police departments that helps foster this problem.”

Viewpoint 5

> *"We are getting a lot of information on officers that do things that we consider to be bad. But we don't have any information on officers who do things that we consider to be good."*

Changing Policing's Misguided Reward Structure Would Put the Focus on Community

Jane Miller and Rashawn Ray

The following viewpoint is a summary of highlights from an expert panel brought together by the Brookings Institution to discuss the state of policing in the U.S. The participants lay out challenges in policing, such as mental health, and suggest ways the institution can be reformed in order to bolster relations between police and the communities they serve. Jane Miller is Public Affairs Intern at the Brookings Institution. Rashawn Ray is Senior Fellow, Governance Studies, at the Brookings Institution, and Professor of Sociology at the University of Maryland, College Park.

"Highlights: Improving Police Culture in America," by Jane Miller and Rashawn Ray, The Brookings Institution, November 4, 2019. Reprinted by permission.

As you read, consider the following questions:

1. According to the viewpoint, why does police training often pit officers against the community they serve?
2. Why is mental health of police officers an important consideration, according to the viewpoint?
3. How can consent decrees help police reform?

In the wake of many high-profile, officer-involved shootings—particularly involving Black Americans—civilians, the media, and politicians have become increasingly critical of American policing. While new policies and technologies have been aimed at addressing public concern, there remains a lot of work to be done to improve the experiences of police officers and police culture.

At an Oct. 25 event, Brookings brought together an expert panel to discuss the state of American policing, as well as the roadblocks and solutions to implementing effective reform. The event featured: Nancy La Vigne, vice president of justice policy at the Urban Institute; Capt. Joe Perez, president of the Hispanic National Law Enforcement Association; and Rashawn Ray, a David M. Rubenstein Fellow at Brookings. Senior Fellow Vanessa Williamson served as moderator.

The event was put on by Brookings's Race, Prosperity, and Inclusion Initiative.

Policing Culture

Experts began the conversation by discussing the biggest challenges facing policing. The panelists agreed many issues stem from the toxic culture fostered by police recruitment, training, and leadership.

Perez, previously a captain of the Prince George's Police Department, described the pattern of "heavy handed" policing that permeates police leadership and training practices. With a significant focus on officer safety, he said police training often pits officers against the community they serve.

La Vigne noted the presence of a "warrior mentality" imbued in police training and recruitment. She said this reputation attracts a subset of individuals who may not always be the best fit to deal with the social work issues prevalent on the front lines of policing.

Ray explained how the organizational structure and culture of policing fuels what he sees as the most detrimental challenge: a lack of transparency and accountability. Policies aimed at reform, including implicit bias training and body camera use, fall short because they don't address the root causes of incidents, such as officer-involved shootings. Other ways of resolving internal policing issues, such as civil payouts, mean taxpayer dollars resolve issues with problem police officers rather than indictment or trial.

Perez also acknowledged the frequent use of internal cover-ups within police departments to protect officers who are habitual offenders of excessive use of force. In referencing recent high-profile incidents, Perez said the officers likely had a history of prior incidents that were swept under the rug. Over the course of his own career, Perez said he observed patterns of cover-up where police leadership would label a repeat offender as a "good worker" or "hard charger" without acting on their behavior. "Had [police] done what we were supposed to do from the beginning, we may have prevented some of these high-profile incidents," Perez said.

The Police Experience

Panelists also discussed the implications of the police officer experience, noting the unique challenges of the job. Perez noted that there is no "one size fits all" for the day-to-day job of a patrol officer, meaning the intensity and frequency of work varies widely. He described how serious situations may arise with barely a moment's notice. "When you're called to these dangerous situations, or for dangerous people or incidents, that's all of a sudden—that's a split second," said Perez. "You could go from zero to one hundred ... in a matter of seconds."

Perez explained that police are often trained to see the community as the enemy. Officers who connect with their community are far less likely to be recognized than those who make many arrests, especially ones involving force.

Ray also acknowledged how data on policing reflect this misguided reward structure. "We are getting a lot of information on officers that do things that we consider to be bad," Ray said. "But we don't have any information on officers who do things that we consider to be good. And that is ultimately what we need because, when it comes to training, we need to be able to replicate some of the characteristics that we see that are positive outcomes."

And while policy changes are being made, little is being done to address the staggering statistics on officer mental health. Ray cited a study saying 80% of officers have some type of chronic stress—with significant amounts of those experiencing suicidal thoughts and/or substance abuse problems. Compounding this, 90% of officers reported being reluctant to seek help due to a stigma associated with therapy. According to Ray, the solution is to normalize mental health care through efforts like requiring that officers visit a psychologist or psychiatrist on a periodic basis.

Reforming the Institution

Throughout the event, the panelists often returned to what can be done to make new policies, such as body cameras, virtual reality training, and data gathering, more effective in police reform.

On the implementation of new technologies, La Vigne said that innovations are most likely to be effective when a police agency is intentional about how these technologies are used, informs the community about them before they're deployed, and carefully trains officers on how and how not to utilize the resources. "By and large, most agencies fall short on one or more of those factors," La Vigne said

Ray added that new policies are often decided upon by senior, front-facing officials, but then left to be executed by lower-level staff who may not have the skillset or people-power to do so.

All three experts acknowledged the potential value in having police departments work with the community they serve, as well as the need for improved federal oversight of policies. They also expressed the positive impact of consent decrees, binding agreements overseen by the courts that can mandate change in police departments.

Periodical and Internet Sources Bibliography

The following articles have been selected to supplement the diverse views presented in this chapter.

David Brooks, "The Culture of Policing Is Broken," The Atlantic, June 16, 2020. https://www.theatlantic.com/ideas/archive/2020/06/how-police-brutality-gets-made/613030/

Nicole Brown Chau, "Police brutality goes 'beyond individual bad apples,' professor says," CBS News, June 11, 2020. https://www.cbsnews.com/news/police-brutality-qualified-immunity-osagie-obasogie/

Amanda Calhoun, "End Police Violence Against Black Americans," The Progressive, May 2, 2022. https://progressive.org/op-eds/end-police-violence-calhoun-220502/

David A. Graham, "The Police Can Still Choose Nonviolence," The Atlantic, May 31, 2020. https://www.theatlantic.com/ideas/archive/2020/05/police-have-break-cycle-violence/612430/

John Hirschauer, "The Sole Justification Offered for the Riots Is a Fiction," National Review, June 2, 2020. https://www.nationalreview.com/2020/06/the-sole-justification-offered-for-the-riots-is-a-fiction/

Sam Levin, "US police have killed nearly 600 people in traffic stops since 2017, data shows," The Guardian, April 21, 2022. https://www.theguardian.com/us-news/2022/apr/21/us-police-violence-traffic-stop-data

Peter Nickeas, "Federal database undercounts deaths caused by police, according to researchers," CNN, September 30, 2021. https://www.cnn.com/2021/09/30/us/study-police-deaths-undercount/index.html

Rashawn Ray, "How can we enhance police accountability in the United States?" Brookings Institution, August 25, 2020. https://www.brookings.edu/policy2020/votervital/how-can-we-enhance-police-accountability-in-the-united-states/

Austin Sarat, "How to Change Lethal Force Rules for Police," The Bulwark, June 10, 2020. https://www.thebulwark.com/how-to-change-lethal-force-rules-for-police/

Cathy Young, "Bad Cops, Bad Narratives," The Bulwark, April 27, 2021. https://www.thebulwark.com/bad-cops-bad-narratives/

OPPOSING VIEWPOINTS® SERIES

Chapter 2

Is America's Criminal Justice System Racist?

Chapter Preface

The history of racism and racial oppression in the United States is deeply intertwined with the history of American law enforcement. Some of the earliest iterations of what would become modern police forces were slave patrols in the pre-Civil War South. And in northern cities like Boston, New York, and Chicago, law enforcement frequently participated (both directly and indirectly) in enforcing the segregation and marginalization of black communities throughout the twentieth century.

More recently, advocates for police and criminal justice reform have pointed to racial profiling by law enforcement and statistics showing disproportionate rates of arrest, incarceration, and even police contact among the black community. Well-documented incidents of police brutality involving white officers' treatment of black suspects have fed the impression that racism persists among the law enforcement community.

But the issue is sometimes more complicated than it might seem on the surface of the debate. For instance, police advocates have suggested that the disproportionate rates of police contact among minority communities could have more to do with socio-economic factors than race. Minority communities are frequently concentrated in low-income neighborhoods, which typically have higher crime rates than more affluent areas. So, the heavier police presence in these areas may represent a sensible response to geographic variations in the crime rate, even when the effect on the ground looks and feels a lot like racism.

Despite the acrimony and disagreement that exists between the pro-police and pro-reform sides of the debate, there seems to be wide agreement on one point: there is very little trust between law enforcement authorities and the black community. That lack of trust has deep historical roots and is likely to remain a salient dynamic in American politics for the foreseeable future.

Viewpoint 1

> *"Law enforcement continues to act in defense of white supremacy, and most often with impunity."*

White Supremacist Ideology Is Inherent in U.S. Law Enforcement

Cloee Cooper

In this viewpoint Cloee Cooper asks whether the comparatively mild police response to the January 6 insurrection at the U.S. Capitol reflects some of the connections between white supremacist groups and the law enforcement community. She also looks at examples of overt racism in police departments and other law enforcement agencies throughout U.S. history. Cloee Cooper is a journalist and Senior Researcher at Political Research Associates whose work focuses on social justice issues in contemporary American society. Her writing has been featured in publications including Alternet, PBS Chicago, Social Justice News Nexus, and Imagine2050.

As you read, consider the following questions:

1. Why might a proactive law enforcement response to the January 6 insurrection be counterproductive?
2. What are some connections between law enforcement and white supremacist culture?

"The Racist History of U.S. Law Enforcement," by Cloee Cooper, The Progressive Magazine, February 22, 2021. Reprinted by permission.

3. What would constitute an effective policy response to racial injustice in America?

The storming of the U.S. Capitol by rightwing insurgents on January 6 highlighted the imminent threat of an emboldened and coordinated far right. This has led many people and institutions to call for a doubling down on more policing and federal funding to address domestic terrorism.

But the insurrection also laid bare the complicity of elected officials and law enforcement within this far-right movement. Underestimating the alignment between law enforcement and the far right reinforces a color blindness that led us here. It can also endorse state violence against people of color and poor people.

So far, we've ignored the key lesson from the summer 2020 racial justice reckoning. Law enforcement continues to act in defense of white supremacy, and most often with impunity. What if we stop turning to a carceral system so ill-equipped to solve the rise of racist violence, and instead, fight for racial justice by investing in communities and social services?

While calls for justice following the murder of George Floyd in Minneapolis on May 25, 2020, transformed city police departments, schools, and catalyzed a massive culture shift, some of those lessons have since been pushed aside. As pundits and officials describe the militants who stormed the Capitol as the nation's most significant terrorism threat, they are using the events of January 6 to justify increased policing and surveillance across the country.

The problem with this is that law enforcement disproportionately arrest and kill people of color and poor people. Perhaps not surprisingly, the mechanisms of repression and policing aimed at suppressing the far right inevitably get turned on communities of color and the left.

In January, The Guardian reported that law enforcement officers are about three times more likely to use force against leftwing versus rightwing protests, with Black Lives Matter demonstrations making up the majority of leftwing protests analyzed. Anti-terrorism legislation passed under President Bill Clinton in the wake of the 1995 Oklahoma City bombing has been disproportionately used against Black communities and immigrants. Since the January 6 insurrection, nearly a fifth of state legislators across the country have advanced bills that criminalize dissent.

Perhaps more importantly, calls for increased policing and surveillance as a solution to far-right insurgencies fail to understand how law enforcement continues to advance systemic white supremacy (through jails, immigration enforcement, and the over-policing and neglect of poor Black neighborhoods).

The truth is, law enforcement agencies have racism and far-right problems of their own. At least thirty-nine off-duty police officers from seventeen states participated in the Capitol insurrection, along with just under a dozen former law enforcement officers, according to news accounts.

Those numbers are negligible relative to the nearly 700,000 full-time law enforcement officers in the United States as of 2019. But the long history of under-reporting acts of racism and vigilante violence by law enforcement should serve as a warning.

During the nearly 100 years of Jim Crow segregation, police officers were known to take off their uniforms in the evening and replace them with their Klan robes, contributing to the lynchings of thousands of Black people with impunity.

Following the end of the Jim Crow era, the United States experienced a white nationalist backlash, with numerous white people—both within and outside of institutions—bemoaning the newly gained rights of communities of color. Law enforcement departments became particular hot spots of racial resentment.

One insidious example of this was the Los Angeles County Sheriff's Department, the nation's largest sheriff's department. Starting in the 1970s, the department developed racist clubs, some of which were criteria for acceptance in the department. The Lynwood Vikings, a neo-Nazi white supremacist gang that swelled in ranks throughout the 1980s and 1990s, eventually cost the department $9 million in fines and training costs to settle lawsuits over racially motivated hostility.

Law enforcement departments continue to directly participate in white supremacist and far-right projects. Political Research Associates has documented a network of widespread alignment between sheriffs and far-right paramilitary across the country that launched during the tenure of the nation's first elected Black President.

The paramilitary aligned network, Constitutional Sheriffs and Peace Officers Association, claimed support from more than 400 sheriffs and law enforcement nationwide at its peak. The leader of the Oath Keepers, a racist militia group, helped found this sheriff's association and maintained a close working relationship. Several of the group's members have been charged by the FBI for their alleged involvement in planning and coordinating the Capitol breach, as well as providing tactical support and security for the riot.

Recent investigations also demonstrate law enforcement's participation in explicitly racist and far-right groups on social media. In 2019, Will Carless at the Center for Investigative Reporting found more than 150 law enforcement officers were actively engaging in explicitly white supremacist, anti-Muslim, and paramilitary Facebook groups. Law enforcement were regularly trading racist memes, advancing anti-Muslim conspiracy theories, and demonstrating their support for far right militia.

Law enforcement sympathy with far-right militias was on display during racial justice protests over the summer of 2020. Political Research Associates documented eleven counts of law enforcement cooperating with far-right organizations demonstrating against the Black Lives Matter movement. The number of incidents is likely far greater than those reported.

Following the 2020 summer of racial justice protests, the Brennan Center for Justice published a report, "Hidden in Plain Sight: Racism, White Supremacy and Far Right Militancy in Law Enforcement." It argues that police reforms aimed at addressing racial bias often miss the point—that law enforcement has membership and affiliation with far-right groups, as well as a culture of racism. Even the FBI warned in a now widely cited 2009 report that law enforcement officials often have "active links" to white supremacist and paramilitary formations.

On January 19, 135 civil and human rights organizations across the country called on Congress to oppose the creation of a new domestic terrorism charge to allegedly go after far-right insurgents. Signed by organizations such as the Arab American Institute, Bend the Arc: Jewish Action, Muslim Advocates, and the NAACP Legal Defense Fund, the letter specifically asked Congress to identify ways to address the white supremacist infiltration of law enforcement.

"The January 6 coup attempt led by white supremacist groups attempting to overturn the will of the American people to choose its leader is a clear example of how pervasive white supremacy is in our society and within the ranks of law enforcement itself," Sherrilyn Ifill, president and director-counsel of the NAACP Legal Defense and Educational Fund, Inc. said in a press release.

Counterterrorism practices are far too often blatantly misused to target and criminalize the very marginalized communities that white supremacists target, noted Maya Berry, executive director of the Arab American Institute. "In an inherently biased criminal legal system, we know how additional legal authorities will be used. They will be used, just as they have previously, to target directly impacted communities, including Black and brown people and religious minorities."

The letter also called on federal agencies to be transparent about their mechanisms and resources for fighting white supremacist violence.

Rather than invest in law enforcement and new surveillance mechanisms to address the rise of white supremacist violence, federal, state, and local governments should invest in structures, movements and institutions that build racial justice. Communities under attack from multiple angles don't need to worry about being more heavily targeted because of the Capitol riot. We need structures of security and care that truly protect all.

VIEWPOINT 2

> *"Class is rarely accounted for in data analyses of fatal police violence, and its inclusion deepens our understanding of who is susceptible to it, across racial lines."*

Race and Class Both Matter When It Comes to Analyzing Police Violence

Meagan Day

In the following viewpoint Meagan Day challenges the arguments offered by some on the right about race and policing. She points specifically to author and commentator Heather Mac Donald's claim that the number of white people killed by police undermines claims of racism in law enforcement and suggests a different interpretation of Heather Mac Donald's statistics. She also examines the history of the Black Lives Matter movement over the past several years. Meagan Day is a political activist, researcher, and editor at Jacobin Magazine. She is author of the 2016 book "Maximum Sunlight" and co-author of the 2020 book "Bigger Than Bernie: How We Go From the Sanders Campaign to Democratic Socialism."

"We're Learning More About the Relationships Between Race, Class, and Police Brutality," by Meagan Day, Jacobin Magazine, June 23, 2020. Reprinted by permission.

As you read, consider the following questions:

1. According to the author, how have Heather Mac Donald and others on the right used misleading statistics to support their arguments about police violence?
2. Why does the author reject the argument that police violence against white people undermines theories of racism in law enforcement?
3. Aside from race, what other relevant demographic factors does the author identify as relevant when it comes to the study of police violence?

Right-wing author and commentator Heather Mac Donald's book *The War on Cops: How the New Attack on Law and Order Makes Everyone Less Safe* was published in 2016, between the first and second waves of Black Lives Matter protests. In it, Mac Donald points to both crime statistics showing high reported rates of black people committing crimes and high numbers of white victims of police killings in order to argue that there is no epidemic of unjustified and disproportionate police violence against black Americans. Mac Donald denounces the Black Lives Matter movement as a "fraud" and a "dangerous distraction."

While the Heritage Foundation, the flagship right-wing think tank, found Mac Donald's book too extreme in places, her work has made an impression on the Right. Charlie Kirk, the founder of the right-wing youth organization Turning Point USA, acknowledged her by name this month in a shaky selfie video recorded in the driver's seat of his car. "Was George Floyd wrongly killed? Yes. Is it a trend? No," Kirk said. He concluded his heated monologue, "Support facts. Support data. Support our country. And support police."

In The War On Cops, Mac Donald even takes pains to defend Darren Wilson, the Ferguson police officer who murdered Michael Brown, bemoaning the "anti-Wilson juggernaut" that couldn't be stopped and lamenting that anti-police rhetoric will "heighten the chances of more Michael Browns attacking officers and getting shot themselves." But her hostile stance toward victims of police violence softens conspicuously in one section. She writes:

The persistent belief that we are living through an epidemic of racially biased police shootings is a creation of selective reporting. In 2015 … the white victims of fatal police shootings included a 50-year-old suspect in a domestic assault in Tuscaloosa, Ala., who ran at the officer with a spoon; a 28-year-old driver in Des Moines, Iowa, who exited his car and walked quickly toward an officer after a car chase; and a 21-year-old suspect in a grocery-store robbery in Akron, Ohio, who had escaped on a bike and who did not remove his hand from his waistband when ordered to do so. Had any of these victims been black, the media and activists would probably have jumped on their stories and added their names to the roster of victims of police racism. Instead, because they are white, they are unknown.

Mac Donald only recounts these appalling stories to further harden her reader against the Black Lives Matter movement. But in the process, and in a deeply reactionary book otherwise entirely devoted to justifying and underscoring the necessity of racist police violence, she inadvertently touches on a real phenomenon: large numbers of white Americans are also killed by police officers every year, unarmed and otherwise. According to a paper published today by the People's Policy Project, Justin Feldman's "Police Killings In The U.S.," of the 6,451 police killings recorded between January 2015 and the present, 3,353 of the individuals killed were white, 1,746 were black, and 1,152 were Latino.

It's important to stress that while more white Americans are killed by police in sheer numbers, white people also make up a majority of the US population and are significantly less likely to be killed by police than black people. Feldman finds that "whites had the lowest overall rate of police killings (3.3 per million) followed by Latinos (3.5 per million). The rate of police killings for the black population was more than double that of whites: 7.9 per million."

Outside the Right's reactionary echo chamber, this reality is well known. But Feldman's paper also introduces a new analytical category, pairing data on police killings with census tract poverty data to estimate the likely socioeconomic status of the deceased. This method is imprecise, but it's a step forward in the general body of research on police killings. Class is rarely accounted for in data analyses of fatal police violence, and its inclusion deepens our understanding of who is susceptible to it, across racial lines.

Feldman found that "the rate of police killings increased as census tract poverty increased," with the level of police killings in the highest-poverty quintile more than three times that of the lowest-poverty quintile. In layman's terms, you're overall more likely to be killed by a police officer if you're working-class or poor. Given this country's long and continuing history of intense racial oppression, it's little surprise that black and Latino people are more likely to live in high-poverty areas than white people: Feldman observes that "median census tract poverty was 9.4% for whites compared to 18.7% for black and 16.8% of Latino individuals."

The paper then examines the relationship between poverty quintile and police killings across racial demographics. What Feldman finds is notable: the correlation between poverty and susceptibility to fatal police violence that exists for white people is much stronger than for black and Latino people. In other words, white people who live in the poorest neighborhoods are at high risk of getting killed by a police officer, but black people are at high risk everywhere.

Feldman concludes by entertaining "a counterfactual scenario in which the distribution of poverty quintiles among black people is equal to that of whites" and found that black people would still be killed by police at much higher rates than white people. The same was not true for Latinos according to his analysis—if they had roughly the same wealth distribution as whites, the rates of death by police would look similar.

We can extrapolate two things from this study. First, a lot of white Americans are killed by police, and class plays a major role in determining which white people are at risk of fatal police violence. Second, while class also accounts in large part for people of color's susceptibility to fatal police violence, it doesn't account for the massively disproportionate rates of police killings of black people in particular—only 28 percent.

Conservatives like Heather Mac Donald want you to think that because cops also kill white people, this means there's nothing wrong with policing in America—that Black Lives Matter is built on a lie and should be wholly disregarded, the practices of the police defended and their honor restored. They're wrong.

Black Lives Matter hinges on a verifiable truth about black people's unique susceptibility to police violence. If the movement succeeds in making American police less intrusive, overbearing, and violent, black Americans will disproportionately benefit. But so too will large numbers of Latinos and poor and working-class white people—not just the hundreds who are killed by police every year but also the millions who are incarcerated, on probation or parole, weighed down by their criminal record, have family behind bars, or are otherwise tethered to our unconscionable criminal justice system.

Feldman's study provides all the more reason to continue building a multiracial working-class mass movement that stands in opposition to both racist police brutality and brutal class stratification. To borrow from Charlie Kirk: Support facts. Support data. Support the protests against police violence. And support the struggle to eliminate the racial and economic inequality that factor so heavily in its distribution.

Viewpoint 3

> *"Through the early 20th century, there were few standards for hiring or training officers."*

From Slave Patrols to Traffic Stops, American Policing Has Been Marked by Racism

Connie Hassett-Walker

In the following viewpoint Connie Hassett-Walker provides a historical overview of the connection between racism and law enforcement in American society. She begins by analyzing how modern police forces evolved from vigilante slave patrols in the pre-Civil War era and traces the racial bias in law enforcement through the early twentieth century and finally to more contemporary signposts like the Rodney King verdict and the murder of Michael Brown in 2014. Connie Hassett-Walker is Assistant Professor of Criminal Justice at Norwich University and a former research associate at the Violence Institute of New Jersey. Her work has been published in the Journal of Ethnicity in Criminal Justice, The Conversation, and the Washington Post.

As you read, consider the following questions:

1. What are some of the differences between early forms of law enforcement in the South vs. those in northern cities like New York and Boston?

"The Racist Roots of American Policing: From Slave Patrols to Traffic Stops," by Connie Hassett-Walker, The Conversation, June 2, 2020. https://theconversation.com/the-racist-roots-of-american-policing-from-slave-patrols-to-traffic-stops-112816.

2. According to the author, why is it important to look at the history of law enforcement as opposed to just the reality on the ground today when we think about reform ideas?
3. What are some of the contemporary statistics that lend support to the notion that there is systemic racism in law enforcement?

Outrage over racial profiling and the killing of African Americans by police officers and vigilantes in recent years helped give rise to the Black Lives Matter movement.

But tensions between the police and black communities are nothing new.

There are many precedents to the Ferguson, Missouri protests that ushered in the Black Lives Matter movement. Those protests erupted in 2014 after a police officer shot unarmed 18-year-old Michael Brown; the officer was subsequently not indicted.

The precedents include the Los Angeles riots that broke out after the 1992 acquittal of police officers for beating Rodney King. Those riots happened nearly three decades after the 1965 Watts riots, which began with Marquette Frye, an African American, being pulled over for suspected drunk driving and roughed up by the police for resisting arrest.

I'm a criminal justice researcher who often focuses on issues of race, class and crime. Through my research and from teaching a course on diversity in criminal justice, I have come to see how the roots of racism in American policing—first planted centuries ago—have not yet been fully purged.

Slave Patrols

There are two historical narratives about the origins of American law enforcement.

Policing in southern slave-holding states had roots in slave patrols, squadrons made up of white volunteers empowered to use vigilante tactics to enforce laws related to slavery. They located and returned enslaved people who had escaped, crushed uprisings led by enslaved people and punished enslaved workers found or believed to have violated plantation rules.

The first slave patrols arose in South Carolina in the early 1700s. As University of Georgia social work professor Michael A. Robinson has written, by the time John Adams became the second U.S. president, every state that had not yet abolished slavery had them.

Members of slave patrols could forcefully enter anyone's home, regardless of their race or ethnicity, based on suspicions that they were sheltering people who had escaped bondage.

The more commonly known precursors to modern law enforcement were centralized municipal police departments that began to form in the early 19th century, beginning in Boston and soon cropping up in New York City, Albany, Chicago, Philadelphia and elsewhere.

The first police forces were overwhelmingly white, male and more focused on responding to disorder than crime.

As Eastern Kentucky University criminologist Gary Potter explains, officers were expected to control a "dangerous underclass" that included African Americans, immigrants and the poor. Through the early 20th century, there were few standards for hiring or training officers.

Police corruption and violence—particularly against vulnerable people—were commonplace during the early 1900s. Additionally, the few African Americans who joined police forces were often assigned to black neighborhoods and faced discrimination on the job. In my opinion, these factors—controlling disorder, lack of adequate police training, lack of nonwhite officers and slave patrol origins—are among the forerunners of modern-day police brutality against African Americans.

Jim Crow Laws

Slave patrols formally dissolved after the Civil War ended. But formerly enslaved people saw little relief from racist government policies as they promptly became subject to Black Codes.

For the next three years, these new laws specified how, when and where African Americans could work and how much they would be paid. They also restricted black voting rights, dictated how and where African Americans could travel and limited where they could live.

The ratification of the 14th Amendment in 1868 quickly made the Black Codes illegal by giving formerly enslaved blacks equal protection of laws through the Constitution. But within two decades, Jim Crow laws aimed at subjugating African Americans and denying their civil rights were enacted across southern and some northern states, replacing the Black Codes.

For about 80 years, Jim Crow laws mandated separate public spaces for blacks and whites, such as schools, libraries, water fountains and restaurants—and enforcing them was part of the police's job. Blacks who broke laws or violated social norms often endured police brutality.

Meanwhile, the authorities didn't punish the perpetrators when African Americans were lynched. Nor did the judicial system hold the police accountable for failing to intervene when black people were being murdered by mobs.

Reverberating Today

For the past five decades, the federal government has forbidden the use of racist regulations at the state and local level. Yet people of color are still more likely to be killed by the police than whites.

The Washington Post tracks the number of Americans killed by the police by race, gender and other characteristics. The newspaper's database indicates that 229 out of 992 of those who died that way in 2018, 23% of the total, were black, even though only about 12% of the country is African American.

Uneven Outcomes

Black Americans are 3.23 times more likely than white Americans to be killed by police, according to a new study by researchers from Harvard T.H. Chan School of Public Health. The researchers examined 5,494 police-related deaths in the U.S. between 2013 and 2017. Rates of deadly police encounters were higher in the West and South than in the Midwest and Northeast, according to the study. Racial disparities in killings by police varied widely across the country, with some metropolitan areas showing very high differences between treatment by race. Black Chicagoans, for example, were found to be over 650% more likely to be killed by police than white Chicagoans.

The wide variance in deaths by police shows how preventable these deaths are, study authors Jaquelyn Jahn and Gabriel Schwartz, recent graduates from the Department of Social and Behavioral Sciences, told UPI in a June 24 article.

The study was published online June 24, 2020 in PLOS ONE.

"Black People More than Three Times as Likely as White People to Be Killed During a Police Encounter," The President and Fellows of Harvard College, June 24, 2020. Reprinted by permission.

Policing's institutional racism of decades and centuries ago still matters because policing culture has not changed as much as it could. For many African Americans, law enforcement represents a legacy of reinforced inequality in the justice system and resistance to advancement—even under pressure from the civil rights movement and its legacy.

In addition, the police disproportionately target black drivers.

When a Stanford University research team analyzed data collected between 2011 and 2017 from nearly 100 million traffic stops to look for evidence of systemic racial profiling, they found that black drivers were more likely to be pulled over and to have their cars searched than white drivers. They also found that the percentage of black drivers being stopped by police dropped after dark when a driver's complexion is harder to see from outside the vehicle.

This persistent disparity in policing is disappointing because of progress in other regards.

There is greater understanding within the police that brutality, particularly lethal force, leads to public mistrust, and police forces are becoming more diverse.

What's more, college students majoring in criminal justice who plan to become future law enforcement officers now frequently take "diversity in criminal justice" courses. This relatively new curriculum is designed to, among other things, make future police professionals more aware of their own biases and those of others. In my view, what these students learn in these classes will make them more attuned to the communities they serve once they enter the workforce.

In addition, law enforcement officers and leaders are being trained to recognize and minimize their own biases in New York City and other places where people of color are disproportionately stopped by the authorities and arrested.

But the persistence of racially biased policing means that unless American policing reckons with its racist roots, it is likely to keep repeating mistakes of the past. This will hinder police from fully protecting and serving the entire public.

VIEWPOINT 4

> *"Curbing racial profiling should be a priority for anyone ... who believe government should be color-blind."*

Racial Profiling Is a Constitutional, Moral, and Sociological Problem

Ilya Somin

In the following viewpoint Ilya Somin writes from a self-described libertarian/conservative perspective on the issue of racial bias in law enforcement. He details the constitutional problems with racial profiling and argues that such tactics erode trust between communities and the police. Somin's perspective provides an interesting complement to the progressive arguments about racism in law enforcement. Ilya Somin is Professor of Law at George Mason University. His research focuses on constitutional law, democratic theory, and federalism, and his writing has been featured in the Yale Law Journal, the Stanford Law Review, the New York Times, and the Washington Post.

As you read, consider the following questions:

1. What are some of the different ways that racial profiling manifests in the course of everyday law enforcement work?
2. Why does the author think that racial profiling should be a major concern for conservatives and libertarians?

"The Problem of Racial Profiling—Why It Matters and What Can Be Done About It," by Ilya Somin, Reason Foundation, August 6, 2020. Reprinted by permission.

3. Why has it been difficult to reduce racial profiling through administrative and policy changes?

The killing of African-American George Floyd by a Minneapolis police officer and the resulting protests have called new attention to a longstanding issue with American law enforcement: widespread racial profiling. In this post, I would like to consider why racial profiling is a serious problem, why it's so hard to end, and what nonetheless can be done to reduce it.

As I use the term, racial profiling denotes a situation where law enforcement officers treat members of one racial group worse than they would be treated in the same situation if they belonged to another group. If a police officer stops, searches, or arrests a black person when a white person in the same situation would be left alone, that's a case of racial profiling. By no means all cases of abusive police behavior qualify as racial profiling. As Jason Brennan and Chris Surprenant describe in a recent book, American police too often use excessive force in cases involving white officers and white suspects, where race, presumably, is not an issue. Even abuses involving minority civilians are not always a result of racial profiling. The wrongdoing officers may sometimes be "equal-opportunity" practitioners of police brutality, who would have done what they did regardless of the suspects' race.

Ending racial profiling would not end all abusive law enforcement behavior. It wouldn't even end all abuses where minorities are victims. But racial profiling is a serious problem nonetheless. It causes real suffering, it's unconstitutional, and it poisons relations between law enforcement and minority communities.

I. Why Racial Profiling Matters

Though racial profiling is far from the only flaw in American law enforcement, it is nonetheless widespread. A 2019 Pew Research Center poll found that 59% of black men and 31% of black women say they have been unfairly stopped by police because of their race. Their perceptions are backed by numerous studies—including many that control for other variables, including underlying crime rates—showing that police often treat blacks and Hispanics more harshly than similarly situated whites.

Almost every black male I know can recount experiences of racial profiling. I readily admit they are not a representative sample. But as a law professor, my African-American acquaintances are disproportionately affluent and highly educated. Working-class blacks likely experience racial profiling even more often.

If you don't trust studies or survey data, consider the testimony of conservative Republican African-American Senator Tim Scott, who has movingly recounted multiple incidents in which he was racially profiled by Capitol police. Even being a powerful GOP politician is not enough for a black man to avoid profiling. Or consider the experiences of right-of-center Notre Dame Law School Dean Marcus Cole. Scott and Cole are not easily dismissed as politically correct "snowflakes" who constantly see racism where none exists.

Most cases of racial profiling do not result in anyone being killed, injured, or even arrested. The police unfairly stop, question, or otherwise harass a minority-group member. But they then let him go, perhaps with a traffic ticket (if it was a vehicle stop). Conservatives are not wrong to point out that the average black person is far more likely to be killed or injured by an ordinary criminal than by a police officer.

But that doesn't mean that racial profiling is trivial or insignificant. Even if one isolated incident might qualify as such, it is painful and degrading if the people who are supposed to "protect and serve" you routinely treat you as a second-class citizen merely based on the color of your skin. And it gets worse if it isn't just about you, because your friends and family get the same treatment.

It is also painful and scary to know that, while racial profiling usually doesn't lead to injury or death, there is always a chance that such an incident could horrifically escalate. When a black man encounters a cop, he often has to worry that the officer might kill or injure him even if he did nothing wrong. Such fear is far less common for whites.

Widespread racial profiling also poisons relationships between police and minority communities. If you (with good reason) believe that cops routinely discriminate against your racial or ethnic group, you are less likely to cooperate with them, report crimes or otherwise presume they are acting in good faith. That creates obvious difficulties for both police and civilians.

Curbing racial profiling should be a priority for anyone—including many conservatives and libertarians—who believe government should be color-blind. I have long argued that anyone who holds such views—as I do myself—cannot tolerate ad hoc exceptions for law enforcement.

If you truly believe that it is wrong for government to discriminate on the basis of race, you cannot ignore that principle when it comes to those government officials who carry badges and guns and have the power to kill and injure people. Otherwise, your position is blatantly inconsistent. Cynics will understandably suspect that your supposed opposition to discrimination only arise when whites are the victims, as in the case of affirmative action preferences in education.

Finally, you have special reason to condemn racial profiling if you are a constitutional originalist (as many conservatives are). Today, most cases under the Equal Protection Clause of the Fourteenth Amendment involve challenges to the constitutionality of laws and regulations that discriminate on the basis of race, or are motivated by such discrimination. But the original meaning of the Clause was centrally focused on unequal enforcement of laws by state and local governments, including the police. That happens when authorities enforce laws against some racial or ethnic groups differently than others, treating some more harshly and others more leniently based on their group identity.

Racial profiling is a paradigmatic example of exactly that problem. Where it occurs, victims are denied equal protection because the very officials who are supposed to provide that protection instead treat them more harshly than members of other groups.

II. Why Racial Profiling Is Hard to Combat

While racial profiling is a serious problem, it's also a very difficult one to curtail. One reason why is that it's often hard to detect. With many types of illegal discrimination, the perpetrators leave a record of their decision-making process that can then be assessed by investigators or used as the basis for a lawsuit. In many, perhaps most, racial profiling cases, the relevant decision was made on the fly by a single person, or a small group. There is no record to refer to, and the officer can easily offer a benign explanation for his or her actions. Indeed, sometimes the officer himself won't know for sure whether he would have done the same thing if the race of the civilian involved was different. That makes racial profiling hard to address by using many of the traditional tools of anti-discrimination law, including lawsuits targeting specific discriminatory actions.

An additional problem is that racial profiling isn't always the result of bigotry, defined as hatred of a given minority group. Some officers really are awful bigots. But many, probably most, who engage in racial profiling are not. They are instead acting on the basis of what economists call "rational stereotyping." Police know that members of some racial or ethnic groups, particularly young black males, have relatively high crime rates compared to members of most other groups. In situations where they have little other information to go on, police therefore view members of these groups with heightened suspicion, and as a result are more likely to stop them, search them, arrest them, or otherwise take aggressive action.

If the officers who profiled Senator Tim Scott had known he was a senator, they would likely have left him alone. But all they knew just from seeing him was that he was a black male, and that led them to believe he was statistically more likely to be a threat than a woman or a member of some other racial group might be.

Racial disparities in crime rates have a variety of causes, including a long history of racism, and flawed government policies of many types. But there is little the average cop on the beat can do to alleviate these causes. He or she instead may focus primarily on the resulting differences in crime rates.

The fact that such behavior is "rational" in the sense of the word used by economists does not make it right. Rather, this is just one of a number of situations where rational decision-making by individuals can lead to a harmful systemic outcome. Racial profiling resulting (in part) from rational stereotyping may be efficient from the standpoint of individual officers trying to cope with uncertainty under pressure. But it harms innocent people, and poisons police-community relations in the long run.

But the fact that racial profiling may often be rational makes it more difficult to root out. Police, after all, are far from the only people who use rational stereotyping as a way to cope with limited information. People of all races and walks of life routinely do so in a wide range of contexts. If you come to a party where you don't know anyone, there is a good chance you will make snap judgments about who to try to talk to, and that those judgments may be influenced by stereotyping based on appearance, including race and gender.

Jesse Jackson, the first prominent African-American presidential candidate, once said "There is nothing more painful to me at this stage in my life than to walk down the street and hear footsteps and start thinking about robbery. Then (I) look around and see someone white and feel relieved." Jackson was relying on rational stereotyping: a white person (at least on that particular street) was statistically less likely to be a robber than an African-American.

The point here is not that rational stereotyping by Jackson or by a party-goer is the moral equivalent of racial profiling by police. Very far from it. The latter is far, far worse, because it causes vastly greater harm and injustice. Rather, these examples help us recognize that rational stereotyping is not confined to bigots, that it is very common human behavior, and that it is therefore very hard to avoid.

When we ask police officers to suppress their instincts and avoid racial profiling—as we should!—we are also asking them to exhibit a level of self-control that most of us often fall short of. The demand here goes well beyond simply asking them to avoid being bigoted thugs. It's asking them to refrain from using a decision-making heuristic that even otherwise well-intentioned people may often resort to.

III. What Can Be Done

While curbing racial profiling is difficult, it is not impossible. Many of the policy reforms that can curtail police abuses more generally will also indirectly reduce racial profiling. Abolishing or limiting qualified immunity can incentivize police to reduce abusive behavior of many kinds, including that which stems from profiling. Police who know they can be sued for wrongdoing are likely to be more careful about racial discrimination. Curtailing the War on Drugs and other laws criminalizing victimless offenses can eliminate many of those confrontations between police and civilians that are especially prone to racial bias. The same goes for curbing the power of police unions, which protect abusive officers of all types, including those who engage in racial discrimination.

If racial profiling is hard to detect, we can at least impose serious punishment in cases where it does get detected. If officers know that racial discrimination is likely to land them in hot water, they may try harder to avoid it, even if the chance of getting caught in any one incident is relatively low.

Perhaps the lowest-hanging fruit is getting rid of the policy under which the federal government explicitly permits the use of racial and ethnic profiling in the enforcement of immigration law in "border" areas (which are defined broadly enough to include locations where some two-thirds of the American population lives). This is by far the most extensive example of openly permitted racial discrimination in federal government policy. The Obama administration decided to let it continue, and Trump has perpetuated it as well. If we are serious about ending racial discrimination in law enforcement, it needs to go.

Laws and incentives are important. But ending racial profiling—like other forms of invidious discrimination—also requires cultural change. Survey data indicate that most white police officers believe current law enforcement practices treat blacks fairly (though the same polls show most minority officers disagree). Many of these officers probably believe racial profiling is justified, or at least defensible under the circumstances police face on the job. That needs to change.

History shows that progress against prejudice and discrimination often depends on changing social norms, as much as on laws. When I was growing up in the 1980s, it was—in most places—socially acceptable to display open bigotry against gays and lesbians. People routinely used words such as "fag" and "homo" as insults—even in liberal Massachusetts (where I lived at the time). People who behave that way today would be socially stigmatized in most settings, even though such expressions remain legal. The stigma is one reason why such behavior is a lot less ubiquitous than it used to be.

Police work is one of the relatively few settings in which widespread racial discrimination—of a certain type—is still considered socially acceptable. If that changes, the behavior itself is likely to change, even if it remains difficult to challenge through formal legal processes. Consider what might happen if police officers known to engage in racial profiling were stigmatized by their peers or by respected authority figures in their communities. In that world, racial profiling would probably still exist; but it would likely be a good deal less common.

I don't have any brilliant suggestions for bringing about such a change in social norms. But history shows it can be done, and the issue is one that deserves more consideration by those with relevant expertise.

In sum, racial profiling is genuine problem that deserves to be taken seriously. There is no simple solution to it. We probably can't get rid of it entirely. But much can be done to make it less widespread than it is today.

Viewpoint 5

> *"If blacks are overrepresented in committing violent crimes, then the likelihood they will be killed by police will be higher as well."*

The Evidence Does Not Support Claims of Systemic Racism in Law Enforcement

Charlemagne Institute

In the following viewpoint the Charlemagne Institute examines five separate claims associated with the progressive Left about racism in law enforcement and rejects each one. Introducing new statistics and stark re-interpretations of relevant research, the author works to undermine the general evidence offered in favor of the claims and to the Left as a bastion of irrationality and confusion when it comes to race issues. The Charlemagne Institute is an educational non-profit organization focused on promoting the celebration of Western values, culture, and civilization and defending the West against contemporary criticism from the Left.

As you read, consider the following questions:

1. How many unarmed white people did the police shoot in 2015?
2. Who is statistically more likely to shoot an unarmed Black suspect: a Black officer or white officer?
3. Why is deemphasizing victims a problem, according to the author?

"The Five Myths of Systemic Racism in Policing," Charlemagne Institute, May 18, 2021. Reprinted by permission.

The belief that law enforcement is infused with systemic racism is a myth. As the evidence demonstrates, blacks are not disproportionately killed by the police. Moreover, the perception of white officers as trigger-happy is also baseless. Here is a rebuttal of five popular lies.

Myth 1: Blacks Are Disproportionately Killed by the Police

Blacks are 13.4 percent of the population yet they account for 48.9 percent of murder offenses, according to 2019 FBI crime statistics. Telling us that they are more likely to be killed by the police relative to their share of the population is irrelevant. Obviously, if blacks are overrepresented in committing violent crimes, then the likelihood they will be killed by police will be higher as well.

The harsh truth is that blacks are disproportionately perpetrators and victims of violent crime. Furthermore, research reveals that since 2015, police have shot and killed 168 unarmed white people, 135 unarmed black people, and 74 unarmed Hispanic people. Since more unarmed whites were killed by the police than unarmed minorities, the logic of activists suggests the real victims of systemic racism are whites.

Myth 2: White Officers Are Trigger-Happy

Researchers have known for a long time that black officers show a greater tendency to shoot unarmed suspects compared to white officers. A possible explanation for the aggression of black officers is that they may more often be stationed in volatile areas requiring greater use of force. Work by the Crime Prevention Research Center compared cities where whites are killed to cities where blacks are killed, and found the latter exhibit higher rates of violent crime on average.

Another issue is that officers are usually situated in communities in which most citizens are of the same race. Hence the findings of

Greg Ridgeway, that black officers are more inclined to employ deadly force, could be driven by these factors:

> Black officers had more than three times greater odds of shooting than white officers. This finding runs counter to concerns that white officers are overrepresented among officers using lethal force and is consistent with several previous studies of officer race and police use-of-force.

Likewise, a 2015 Philadelphia Police Department study found that black officers were 67 percent more likely than their white peers to mistakenly shoot an unarmed black suspect. John Lott is the latest researcher to confirm these results.

Myth 3: Police Officers Employ Unjustified Force

Commentators tend to paint police officers as aggressive. However, the truth is that they often exercise restraint even while enduring abuse.

An officer is far more likely to be a victim of an assault than is a perpetrator. In one year, 2014, there were more than 48,000 assaults on police officers reported to the FBI, and that was only counting two-thirds of law enforcement agencies, criminal justice expert Dr. Richard Johnson reports. More than a quarter of those assaults resulted in an injury to the officer requiring medical treatment. Johnson goes on to estimate that only one citizen death occurred for every 10 deadly weapon attacks on officers—those in which the citizen assaulted the officer with a gun, blade, blunt object, or moving vehicle.

Judging by the data it is evident that police officers display immense self-control even in adverse situations.

Myth 4: De-policing Is Good for Black Communities

When politically motivated decisions erode police authority, crime is likely to escalate, not decrease as some would argue. Tanaya Devi and Roland G. Fryer Jr. posit in a 2020 study that investigations of police brutality that were sparked by nationwide sensational media coverage produce unintended consequences.

> For the five investigations that were sparked by nationally visible incidents of deadly use of force—Baltimore, Chicago, Cincinnati, Ferguson and Riverside—investigations cause statistically significant increases in both homicide and total crime.

The authors contend that these sensational investigations undermined the authority of police departments, and as a result de-policing led to increases in crime.

Myth 5: Progressive Criminal Reform Benefits Blacks

Presently, activists fixate on minimizing punishment for offenders either by decriminalizing certain activities or reducing sentencing. But one bold reformer Daniel Fryer admits that by de-emphasizing the plight of victims, progressives are doing a disservice to blacks. Relying on the wisdom of James Forman, Fryer argues that in the 1960s, blacks felt that applying a "less rigorous standard of law enforcement in the ghetto," by tolerating illicit activities, was a violation of their civil rights.

The conclusion to Fryer's paper is quite sobering:

> If all of this is right, any decarceration program that does not make a conscious effort to avoid the devaluation of black victims will contain the potential to be abused and applied in a biased manner. We cannot forget that leniency is sometimes regarded as the common way in which a state expresses that black lives don't matter.

Systemic racism is refuted by the evidence. Instead of promoting senseless claims, liberals should steer blacks away from crime. Simply encouraging them to distrust the police, in the absence of evidence, is a recipe for disaster.

Periodical and Internet Sources Bibliography

The following articles have been selected to supplement the diverse views presented in this chapter.

ACLU, "What 100 Years of History Tells Us About Racism in Policing," ACLU News, December 11, 2020. https://www.aclu.org/news/criminal-law-reform/what-100-years-of-history-tells-us-about-racism-in-policing

Radley Balko, "There's overwhelming evidence that the criminal justice system is racist. Here's the proof," The Washington Post, June 10, 2020. https://www.washingtonpost.com/graphics/2020/opinions/systemic-racism-police-evidence-criminal-justice-system/

Zack Beauchamp, "What the Police Really Believe," Vox, July 7, 2020. https://www.vox.com/policy-and-politics/2020/7/7/21293259/police-racism-violence-ideology-george-floyd

Laura Bronner, "Why Statistics Don't Capture the Full Extent of the Systemic Bias in Policing," FiveThirtyEight, June 25, 2020. https://fivethirtyeight.com/features/why-statistics-dont-capture-the-full-extent-of-the-systemic-bias-in-policing/

Michael German, "Hidden in Plain Sight: Racism, White Supremacy, and Far-Right Militancy in Law Enforcment," Brennan Center, August 27, 2020. https://www.brennancenter.org/our-work/research-reports/hidden-plain-sight-racism-white-supremacy-and-far-right-militancy-law

Ken Gordon, "Protests marking killings of Black people also are about much bigger societal issues," The Columbus Dispatch, April 18, 2021. https://www.dispatch.com/story/news/local/2021/04/18/systemic-racism-police-brutality-against-black-people-drive-protests/7226189002/

John McWhorter, "What's Missing from the Conversation About Systemic Racism," The New York Times, September 28, 2021. https://www.nytimes.com/2021/09/28/opinion/redlining-systemic-racism.html

Lynne Peeples, "What the data say about police brutality and racial bias—and which reforms might work," Nature, June 19, 2020. https://www.nature.com/articles/d41586-020-01846-z

Colleen Walsh, "Solving Racial Disparities in Policing," The Harvard Gazette, February 23, 2021. https://news.harvard.edu/gazette/story/2021/02/solving-racial-disparities-in-policing/

Justin Worland, "America's Long Overdue Awakening to Systemic Racism," Time, June 11, 2020. https://time.com/5851855/systemic-racism-america/

OPPOSING VIEWPOINTS® SERIES

CHAPTER 3

Should the U.S. Ban Qualified Immunity for Law Enforcement Officers?

Chapter Preface

One of the more specific issues within the larger debate on police reform concerns the doctrine of qualified immunity, which shields police officers and other public officials from liability when it comes to actions taken as part of their official duties. Police advocates have defended qualified immunity on the basis that it protects law enforcement officers from frivolous lawsuits. Critics argue that it places police officers above the law.

The scope of qualified immunity in American jurisprudence has been shaped by a number of important court decisions over the past several decades. The current case law sets a difficult standard for plaintiffs, in that they must demonstrate that accused law enforcement officers' actions were illegal according to "clearly established law" and that the officers knew this to be the case. This standard, which dates to the 1982 Supreme Court decision *Harlow v. Fitzgerald*, has significantly expanded the scope of qualified immunity defenses in cases involving police brutality and misconduct.

Qualified immunity is one of the few areas of the police reform debate where observers from across the political spectrum have found common ground. Supreme Court Justices Sonia Sotomayor and Clarence Thomas, who couldn't be further apart on an ideological plane, have both questioned the constitutionality of the doctrine. Conservatives often tend to concentrate on the pro-law enforcement side of the discussion, but libertarian-leaning conservatives who are largely concerned with state power and individual liberty have criticized the way that qualified immunity has expanded police power and allowed for the proliferation of highly intrusive law enforcement techniques.

The debate over qualified immunity in U.S. law points directly at many of the most controversial elements of the larger conversation on police reform and is likely to play a central role in any major legislative reform efforts in the years ahead.

Viewpoint 1

> *"The central friction is whether it is reasonable to ask police to enforce the law without protection from frivolous lawsuits ..."*

Qualified Immunity Is a Sticking Point in the Police Reform Debate

Al Tompkins

In the following viewpoint Al Tompkins explores the recent history of the debates around qualified immunity for law enforcement officers in the United States. He examines some of the legal arguments for and against the doctrine from groups and also looks at some of the public figures who have expressed their political support for reforming the law to allow for more accountability from police officers. Al Tompkins is a journalist, producer, and news director. He is currently a Senior Faculty for Broadcast and Online at the Poynter Institute.

As you read, consider the following questions:

1. What two elements must plaintiffs demonstrate in order to open a police office to a civil lawsuit?
2. What key questions have Supreme Court justices raised in terms of the constitutionality of qualified immunity?
3. What are the arguments about qualified immunity that have united both liberal and conservative groups against it?

"What Is 'Qualified Immunity' for Police and Why Are There Calls to End It?" by Al Tompkins, The Poynter Institute, June 15, 2020. Reprinted by permission.

Congress is kicking around ideas for reforming police departments. A key sticking point is the notion of "qualified immunity," a legal doctrine that keeps police officers safe from civil lawsuits. Democrats want to end qualified immunity for police, but Republicans say that idea goes too far.

The central friction is whether it is reasonable to ask police to enforce the law without protection from frivolous lawsuits—while that very protection may enable police to overreact and abuse people without the fear of being sued.

Nearly every year for the last decade, the Supreme Court has taken up at least one case involving qualified immunity for police and nearly always rules in favor of police.

Justices Sonia Sotomayor and Clarence Thomas, on different ends of the political spectrum, have each written about the dangers of qualified immunity. In a 2018 ruling, Sotomayor wrote that with the immunity, police can "shoot first and think later, and it tells the public that palpably unreasonable conduct will go unpunished." Justice Thomas has said qualified immunity has no historical basis and was invented by judges. In 2017, Justice Thomas wrote about his "growing concern with our qualified immunity jurisprudence."

Reuters recently published a special report on this issue. Reuters looked at 252 cases from 2015 to 2019 where plaintiffs sought to abolish qualified immunity for the police that they wanted to sue. In about half of those cases, the courts upheld the qualified immunity that protected the officers.

Reuters found that since 2005, the courts have shown "an increasing tendency to grant immunity in excessive force cases.

The Two-Part Test to Overcome Immunity

Generally, when a plaintiff wants to remove qualified immunity and open a police officer to a civil lawsuit, the plaintiff must meet a two-part test:

1. They must show evidence that a jury would be likely to find the officer's use of force would violate the Fourth Amendment.

2. They must show that the officers should have known they were violating "clearly established law."

The Legal Information Institute at the Cornell Law School offers useful background:

> "Qualified immunity balances two important interests—the need to hold public officials accountable when they exercise power irresponsibly and the need to shield officials from harassment, distraction, and liability when they perform their duties reasonably." *Pearson v. Callahan.*
>
> Specifically, qualified immunity protects a government official from lawsuits alleging that the official violated a plaintiff's rights, only allowing suits where officials violated a "clearly established" statutory or constitutional right. When determining whether or not a right was "clearly established," courts consider whether a hypothetical reasonable official would have known that the defendant's conduct violated the plaintiff's rights. Courts conducting this analysis apply the law that was in force at the time of the alleged violation, not the law in effect when the court considers the case.
>
> Qualified immunity is not immunity from having to pay money damages, but rather immunity from having to go through the costs of a trial at all. Accordingly, courts must resolve qualified immunity issues as early in a case as possible, preferably before discovery.
>
> Qualified immunity only applies to suits against government officials as individuals, not suits against the government for damages caused by the officials' actions. Although qualified immunity frequently appears in cases involving police officers, it also applies to most other executive branch officials. While judges, prosecutors, legislators, and some other government officials do not receive qualified immunity, most are protected by other immunity doctrines.

Professional Athletes Got Involved

More than 1,400 former and current MLB, NBA and NFL athletes (see the list), including quarterbacks Tom Brady and Drew Brees, signed a petition supporting the Democratic version of the police reform bill that would end qualified immunity. The athletes wrote:

> The Supreme Court has caused irreparable harm to public trust by creating and then expanding the doctrine of qualified immunity, which often exempts police officers and others from liability, even for shocking abuse. Under that doctrine, first developed in 1967 and widened ever since, plaintiffs must show that government officials violated "clearly established" law to receive damages for harm. A plaintiff wins only if a prior Court found an official liable under a nearly identical fact-pattern. This standard is virtually impossible to meet, and the protections promised under section 1983 seem largely symbolic as a result.
>
> Qualified immunity has shielded some of the worst law enforcement officials in America. The 8th Circuit applied it to an officer who wrapped a woman in a bear hug, slammed her to the ground, and broke her collarbone as she walked away from him. The 9th Circuit applied the doctrine to two officers who allegedly stole $225,000 while executing a search warrant. The Eleventh Circuit applied the doctrine to protect an officer who unintentionally shot a 10-year-old while firing at the family dog (who, much like the child, posed no threat). The list of officers who suffered no consequences because of this doctrine could fill a law book.

The Legislation That Will Come This Week

Even as Congress is politically divided over this issue, a wide range of political players have lined up in favor of reform. Reuters found many groups—including the American Civil Liberties Union, Cato Institute, NAACP Legal Defense Fund and the conservative Alliance Defending Freedom—are involved in cases fighting qualified immunity for police.

Republicans plan to propose a police reform bill this week, but Republican Sen. Tim Scott of South Carolina said abolishing qualified immunity won't have enough support to make the final package. The White House said it will not support legislation that removes qualified immunity for police.

The Hill reported:

> Qualified immunity, developed through a handful of Supreme Court rulings, protects police officers from being held personally liable if their actions do not violate a "clearly established" law. There are currently eight cases related to qualified immunity under consideration by the Supreme Court, though justices would need to agree to hear the cases. Justices Clarence Thomas and Sonia Sotomayor have both voiced skepticism about the legal doctrine.
>
> Critics argue that its intent, to protect police officers from frivolous lawsuits, has instead been stretched to make it difficult for someone to sue a police officer even in cases where they believe there are clear examples of excessive force or violations of civil rights.

The Democrat-backed "Justice in Policing Act" includes a ban on chokeholds, a ban on racial profiling and ends "no-knock" warrants. It requires police to wear body cameras and would limit the transfer of military-grade equipment to police departments. It also:

> Requires that deadly force be used only as a last resort and requires officers to employ de-escalation techniques first. Changes the standard to evaluate whether law enforcement use of force was justified from whether the force was "reasonable" to whether the force was "necessary."

But the ban on qualified immunity may be the most controversial part of this sweeping legislation. Read the bill here. Here is what it says:

> Section 1979 of the Revised Statutes of the United 16 States (42 U.S.C. 1983) is amended by adding at the end the following: "It shall not be a defense or immunity to any action brought under this section against a local law enforcement officer (as defined in section 2 of the Justice in Policing Act of 2020) or a

> State correctional officer (as defined in section 1121(b) of title 18, United States Code) that—"(1) the defendant was acting in good faith, or that the defendant believed, reasonably or otherwise, that his or her conduct was lawful at the time when the conduct was committed; or "(2) the rights, privileges, or immunities secured by the Constitution and laws were not clearly established at the time of their deprivation by the defendant, or that at this time, the state of the law was otherwise such that the defendant could not reasonably have been expected to know whether his or her conduct was lawful."

Local Angles

Your local police union will have a lot to say about this issue. Officers will tell you they cannot do their job without some level of protection from lawsuits. Local plaintiff lawyers will tell you about why they don't take cases involving police abuse because of the high bar they must overcome to avoid the immunity that protects police.

Of course, ask your local members of Congress where they fall on the legislation that is taking shape this week. Get candidates on the record.

There are so many local cases to explore, including a couple that the Supreme Court recently rejected for consideration. Here are links to those, which also contain contact information for the attorneys who are involved:

- (Wymore, Nebraska) Kelsay v. Ernst, U.S., No. 19-682, review denied May 18
- (Fresno, California) Jessop v. City of Fresno, U.S., No. 19-1021, review denied May 18

VIEWPOINT 2

> *"An aggrieved citizen with a civil rights complaint can no longer argue that an officer's conduct was motivated by wrongful intent, malice or even prejudice."*

It May Be Time to End Qualified Immunity for Law Enforcement Officers

Ronnie R. Gipson Jr.

In the following viewpoint Ronnie R. Gipson Jr. examines the legal history of both absolute and qualified immunity in American jurisprudence since the 1700s. He then places the legal history of immunity in the context of contemporary debates on police violence, racism in the justice system, and the politics of police labor unions. Finally, he looks at the steps that some states and local jurisdictions have taken since the murder of George Floyd to limit qualified immunity for law enforcement officers. Ronnie R. Gipson Jr. is Professor of Law at the University of Memphis Law School.

As you read, consider the following questions:

1. What are the differences between absolute immunity and qualified immunity in the U.S. legal system?

2. How has the doctrine of qualified immunity been expanded by court rulings?
3. What are the current standards that can open a law enforcement officer to liability in the context of a civil lawsuit?

When police officers kill people without apparent justification, those officers may face both criminal charges—as in the case of Derek Chauvin, convicted of murdering George Floyd in Minneapolis in 2020—and civil lawsuits.

Floyd's family filed a federal civil rights suit against Chauvin and three other officers, alleging they used "unjustified, excessive, illegal and deadly force" while detaining him. The suit also named the city of Minneapolis, alleging city officials did not have good policies about using force and didn't train the officers properly.

In March 2021, as Chauvin's criminal trial was set to begin, the city settled the lawsuit—agreeing to pay US$27 million to Floyd's family—but Chauvin and the other officers paid nothing.

That's because, as a Minneapolis police officer at the time he killed Floyd, Chauvin was legally immune from civil lawsuits seeking damages for his actions. The principle is called "qualified immunity," and it protects government workers from being sued for things they do in their official roles at work.

A Brief History of Immunity

The U.S. legal system has two types of immunity. The first is absolute immunity, which has a long history dating back to judges' rulings under English common law from the 1700s. This type of immunity protects judges and lawmakers from being sued by people who suffer financially from their rulings or policy decisions. Therefore, judges and lawmakers are free to make the best decisions for society as a whole without worrying that anyone who is somehow harmed by their choices could come back and sue them for damages.

The second kind of immunity, the one that affects police officers, stems from the Civil Rights Act of 1871. That law allowed an officer to be sued for official acts only if he knew, or should have known, that his action would violate a person's constitutional rights, or if he intended to deprive someone of their constitutional rights. This liability depended on the officer's internal state of mind, which is notoriously hard to prove in court.

In 1967, the U.S. Supreme Court changed that focus. The change came about in a ruling that an officer could not be sued for false arrest in the arrest of a person who was later found not to be guilty of a crime. The court did not look at the officer's state of mind. Instead, the court compared the officer's actions with those that would be taken by a reasonable public official in the same circumstances. If the officer's actions were reasonable, then immunity was granted.

Over time, this immunity has been expanded by the courts. It now extends to cover other misdeeds, such as infringement of a suspect's civil rights during the exercise of a police officer's authority, whether those misdeeds were intentional or not.

Making Lawsuits Harder

The current standard, created by the Supreme Court in 1982, protects officers from being sued in civil court unless their actions are objectively ruled a violation of the law.

An aggrieved citizen with a civil rights complaint can no longer argue that an officer's conduct was motivated by wrongful intent, malice or even prejudice. What matters is not what the officer did but how it compares with what a reasonable officer might have done.

The result of the changed standard has been to severely limit the number of civil claims against police that make it past the officer's broad defense of qualified immunity.

Over many decades, and with increasing intensity in recent years, news reports and citizen complaints have identified police officers harming civilians, particularly Black Americans, seemingly

Qualified Immunity

Qualified immunity is a judicially established doctrine designed to protect public officials from liability when performing acts necessary in their job. This complex doctrine has continued to be a topic of controversy in today's political climate. For those working within the government sphere, qualified immunity is generally perceived as a necessary protection for normal business function. For those outside of the government sphere, qualified immunity may be viewed as a protection that enables some civil servants to commit acts that that harm others without appropriate consequences.

Government attorneys most typically encounter cases that involve qualified immunity in cases related to state or federal officials, law enforcement officials, teachers, or social workers.

History of Qualified Immunity

- 1871: The Supreme Court developed the origins of qualified immunity with their interpretation of the Civil Rights Act of 1871, Section 1983. The Civil Rights Act of 1871 was originally intended to broaden the government's ability to combat attacks perpetrated against African Americans by the Ku Klux Klan and other white supremacy groups.
- 1967: The Supreme Court ruling in Pierson v. Ray held that the "Good Faith Defense" was available to protect a public official challenged under Section 1983.
- 1982: In Harlow v. Fitzgerald, the Supreme Court refocused its definition of qualified immunity to assess the objective legality of a public official's actions, rather than assessing the subjective intent of the official. The court held that an official could have immunity "insofar as their conduct does not violate clearly established statutory or constitutional rights of which a reasonable person would have known."
- 2020: In the Taylor v. Riojas ruling, the Supreme Court removed qualified immunity as a protection for the actions of correctional officers.

"Qualified Immunity," National Association of Attorneys General.

with impunity. Officers know the law will shield them from personal liability, and they also know that it is rare for officers to face criminal charges—much less be convicted.

But recent examples may bring additional attention to this issue.

In March 2021, Marion Humphrey, a Black law student at the University of Arkansas, filed a federal lawsuit against an Arkansas state trooper, alleging the trooper unlawfully searched his personal belongings during a traffic stop in August 2020. The trooper has not been disciplined or faced criminal changes, but the lawsuit says a video camera captured the trooper making insulting remarks about Humphrey's race and age.

In April 2021, Caron Nazario, a Black U.S. Army lieutenant, filed a civil rights lawsuit against two police officers in Virginia who pepper-sprayed him during a December 2020 traffic stop. One of the officers involved was fired, and the other was ordered to undergo retraining. The state attorney general is investigating the incident, in which Nazario says his constitutional rights were violated.

It is not yet clear how those lawsuits will address the possibility of the officers claiming—or being granted—qualified immunity. But those incidents and others like them have sparked intense debate about whether, and under what circumstances, police officers should have qualified immunity.

Proponents say qualified immunity offers a balance between letting victims hold officials accountable and minimizing harm to society as a whole. Opponents say it serves as protection for wrongdoers that harks back to Jim Crow laws and is a vestige of racism that perpetuates unequal treatment before the law.

A Move to Eliminate Qualified Immunity

Qualified immunity is a federal law construct; however, some states are already moving to do away with this type of legal protection for police officers. In June 2020, the state of Colorado did so, in direct response to George Floyd's death and the resulting protests. In August 2020, Connecticut took a similar step.

In March 2021, the New York City Council did the same for its police department. New Mexico joined the growing movement the following month.

At the federal level, the U.S. House of Representatives passed the George Floyd Justice in Policing Act in March 2021, which in part seeks to limit the ability of police officers to claim qualified immunity as a defense in private lawsuits. The bill is now in the U.S. Senate for consideration. Similar laws are likely to spread across the country as Americans and their lawmakers examine whether qualified immunity for police does more harm than good.

VIEWPOINT 3

> *"Qualified immunity does not elevate police officers above the law, nor does it make it impossible to sue an officer for violating your rights."*

In Defense of Qualified Immunity

Tom Cotton

In the following viewpoint Tom Cotton argues that qualified immunity is an essential protection for police officers, among other government employees, to do their jobs without fear of frivolous but impactful lawsuits. Cotton also contends that most people do not understand that qualified immunity is, as the term makes explicit, qualified. It does not, in fact, shield bad police from misconduct. Tom Cotton is a US senator, representing the state of Arkansas.

As you read, consider the following questions:

1. According to the author, what does qualified immunity shield police officers from?
2. What has the Supreme Court ruled regarding qualified immunity?
3. What does the author predict would result from eliminating qualified immunity?

"In Defense of Qualified Immunity," by Tom Cotton, National Review, October 27, 2021. Reprinted by permission.

Qualified immunity is essential to effective and diligent policing. It shields good police officers from bankruptcy while still subjecting individual bad actors to personal financial repercussions. Any effort to abolish or significantly curtail this indispensable protection is a veiled attempt to defund, defame, and disarm the police in the midst of the worst violent-crime wave in a generation.

Qualified immunity safeguards police officers from personal lawsuits, unless they engage in behavior that they reasonably should have known violated a citizen's rights. This protects officers from malicious lawsuits that would otherwise financially cripple them and hollow out departments.

Shielding civil servants from vindictive personal lawsuits is a common practice. Most government employees enjoy the same or similar protections. Park rangers, DMV clerks, judges, sanitation workers, and elected officials are all granted some level of immunity—despite the fact that none of them have to make nearly as many split-second and life-changing decisions as police officers.

Contrary to the misinformed and disingenuous arguments of critics, qualified immunity does not elevate police officers above the law, nor does it make it impossible to sue an officer for violating your rights. It is, by definition, "qualified," limited, and conditional. As the Supreme Court held in 1986, it does not protect "the plainly incompetent or those who knowingly violate the law." A rogue officer who brutally beats a suspect or manufactures evidence, for example, can be held personally liable and sued for his actions.

Qualified immunity leaves ample room for accountability, and plaintiffs regularly prevail in court. In 43 percent of cases alleging excessive force between 2017–2019, courts held that the officers' unreasonable actions placed them outside the bounds of qualified-immunity protections.

There are also many other ways to hold officers to a high standard and get justice for victims of police mistakes and malfeasance. Officers who violate department policies can be disciplined or fired, and those who commit crimes are criminally prosecuted just like anyone else. Victims of police errors or crimes also often receive financial compensation from the department or by suing the city government. Personal lawsuits are far from necessary to ensure justice and accountability.

While some activists have attempted to use the tragic death of George Floyd as a hook for their anti–qualified-immunity activism, they ignore that the officer involved, Derek Chauvin, faced criminal prosecution for his actions and Floyd's family received a $27 million settlement from the city. In fact, the Chauvin case proves the opposite of what critics claim.

Eliminating qualified immunity would result in far less accountability and democratic control over law enforcement. Without this protection, police would be forced to procure private insurance against personal lawsuits. This would not only increase the cost of policing but would also put insurance companies in a position to dictate enforcement practices and activity. Insurance companies would inevitably demand that states and cities curtail policing practices that expose officers to higher liability, in order to avoid higher costs and risks for the company. Insurance executives would thereby undemocratically shape public safety and set policy on behalf of Americans living in dangerous neighborhoods. All the while, plaintiffs with legitimate claims would have to face off against insurance-company lawyers—who are motivated by profit, not justice or fairness.

In all likelihood, the practical result of eliminating or significantly curtailing qualified immunity would be fewer police, less enforcement, and more crime. This is the true goal of most critics of qualified immunity. They are seeking to covertly "defund the police" without ever saying those words. They must not succeed.

When police officers strap on their guns and vests, and put their lives at risk to protect the people in their community, they shouldn't have to worry about financial ruin just for doing their job. We should protect those who protect us—and that means protecting qualified immunity.

Viewpoint 4

> *"Should an officer become liable if he or she makes an arrest for a violation of a criminal statute that a court later determines was unconstitutional?"*

Qualified Immunity Is a More Complex Issue Than the Current Debate Suggests

Carl J. Schuman

In the following viewpoint Carl J. Schuman delves into the legal complexities surrounding the issue of qualified immunity for law enforcement officers. He draws on his long experience on the bench to describe some of the grey areas around constitutional rights, law enforcement procedure, and civil litigation that can impact lawsuits involving police officers. His perspective offers a counterpoint to the stridently pro-police vs. pro-reform arguments that dominate the public debate over qualified immunity. Carl J. Schuman is a judge for the New Britain District Superior Court in Connecticut and editor of the journal Connecticut Criminal Procedure. He previously served as both an Assistant State Attorney General and Assistant United States Attorney in Connecticut.

"Qualified Immunity for Police Officers: Is There a Middle Ground?" by Carl J. Schuman, Divided We Fall, September 14, 2020. Reprinted from Divided We Fall by Permission. https://dividedwefall.org/qualified-immunity-for-police-officers-is-there-a-middle-ground/

As you read, consider the following questions:

1. What does the *Jamison v. McClendon* case illustrate about the contemporary state of the qualified immunity doctrine in the legal community?
2. Why does the author believe that qualified immunity has a role in American jurisprudence, even though it currently can lead to unjust results?
3. What are some of the difficulties when it comes to reviewing qualified immunity defenses in cases involving excessive force?

The recent death of George Floyd and the shooting of Jacob Blake, as well as other apparent incidents of police misconduct, have sparked a nationwide debate about police reform. One of the more esoteric issues is that of "qualified immunity" of police officers from lawsuit. What is qualified immunity and what, if anything, should we do about it? Is there any room for bipartisan agreement on the issue? Let me explain.

Qualified Immunity

Qualified immunity is a legal doctrine that allows police officers and other governmental officials to avoid civil legal liability if their actions were in good faith. It does not prevent police officers from getting sued. In America, with few exceptions, almost anyone can file a lawsuit against anyone else. But when someone does file a lawsuit against police officers, the officers can raise the defense of "qualified immunity" to prevent a money judgment from entering against them and, in many cases, to avoid having to stand trial.

In federal cases, qualified immunity is a judge-made doctrine largely stemming from twentieth century U.S. Supreme Court cases. Some states, like Connecticut, have recently codified their qualified immunity doctrine for purposes of lawsuits arising under state law. In either case, the main purpose of the doctrine is to protect law enforcement officers from liability when they have made difficult decisions about arrests or searches and have at least a good faith belief that their actions have conformed to existing court decisions in similar situations. Courts and legislators have recognized that most police officers are not lawyers but, nonetheless, are regularly called upon to interpret and follow court decisions while on dangerous assignments. In many cases, officers have to make split second judgments in which someone's life, including their own, is on the line. A limitation on liability through the qualified immunity rule is not unlike what many doctors or other professionals have when they follow the standard of care but there is a bad outcome. The qualified immunity doctrine is also important in the recruitment and retention of competent law enforcement officers.

Jamison v. McClendon

A recent federal case out of the Southern District of Mississippi has brought to light some of the shortcomings of the doctrine. In Jamison v. McClendon, 2020 WL 4497723 (S.D. Miss. Aug. 4, 2020), a white police officer, Nick McClendon, stopped a black driver, Clarence Jamison, driving a Mercedes convertible because his temporary license tag was allegedly folded over. Jamison was driving home to South Carolina from a vacation in Arizona. McClendon detained Jamison for approximately one hour and fifty minutes, repeatedly asked him for consent to search his car, lied to him that he believed that there was a large stash of cocaine in the car, and then, when Jamison consented to a search, did several thousand dollars of damage to the car's seats and convertible top in searching for drugs. Nothing was found.

When Jamison sued McClendon under the federal civil rights laws and McClendon filed a motion raising a qualified immunity defense, United States District Judge Carleton Reeves wrote a long, powerful critique of the qualified immunity doctrine. Judge Reeves explained that, under the current state of the law, an officer can succeed on a qualified immunity defense unless his or her actions violate "clearly established" law, as interpreted by the courts. Judge

The Supreme Court Sides with Police

On Monday, the U.S. Supreme Court ruled that two officers in separate cases should be granted qualified immunity, The Hill reported. Qualified immunity is a legal doctrine that shields government officials from liability.

The ruling reversed two federal appeals court decisions that had allowed excessive force lawsuits against the officers to proceed, according to the report. The two cases, one in California and one in Oklahoma, involved police responses to 911 calls.

In the California case, Officer Daniel Rivas-Villegas responded to a report of a man threatening his girlfriend and her children with a chainsaw. The officer confronted the suspect, placing his knee on the suspect's back for eight seconds while another officer placed the suspect under arrest. An appeals court ruled that the officer wasn't entitled to qualified immunity because "existing precedent put him on notice that his conduct constituted excessive force." The Supreme Court overturned that decision, ruling that the precedent was too different for Rivas-Villegas to have received "fair notice" that his actions were excessive force, according to the report.

In the Oklahoma case, officers responded to a call from a woman who said her ex-husband was intoxicated and refused to leave her garage. Officers shot and killed the man after he threatened officers with a hammer and refused to drop it. An appeals court ruled that the officers had created the deadly situation by "cornering" the suspect, according to The Hill. The Supreme Court reversed that decision, saying that officers were entitled to qualified immunity because the court hadn't noted "a single precedent finding a Fourth Amendment violation under similar circumstances," the report says.

"U.S. Supreme Court sides with police in qualified immunity cases," by Suzie Ziegler, Police 1 By Lexipol, October 19, 2021.

Reeves reluctantly acknowledged that "[t]his Court is required to apply the law as stated by the Supreme Court. Under that law, the officer who transformed a short traffic stop into an almost two-hour, life-altering ordeal is entitled to qualified immunity. The officer's motion seeking as much is therefore granted."

Judge Reeves concluded: "Viewing the facts in the light most favorable to Jamison, the question in this case is whether it was clearly established that an officer who has made five sequential requests for consent to search a car, lied, promised leniency, and placed his arm inside of a person's car during a traffic stop while awaiting background check results has violated the Fourth Amendment. It is not." The Fourth Amendment protects Americans from unreasonable search and seizure. But, Judge Reeves found that there were no appellate cases clearly holding that what Officer McClendon had done was illegal. Therefore, Officer McClendon was entitled to qualified immunity and the court had to dismiss the claims against him for violation of Jamison's civil rights. (For technical reasons, however, Jamison will still be able to go to trial to attempt to recover for the damage to his car.)

In the course of the opinion, however, Judge Reeves commented: "[L]et us not be fooled by legal jargon. Immunity is not exoneration. And the harm in this case to one man sheds light on the harm done to the nation by this manufactured doctrine." Judge Reeves added that "a review of our qualified immunity precedent makes clear that the Court has dispensed with any pretense of balancing competing values. Our courts have shielded a police officer who shot a child while the officer was attempting to shoot the family dog; prison guards who forced a prisoner to sleep in cells 'covered in feces' for days; police officers who stole over $225,000 worth of property; a deputy who body-slammed a woman after she simply 'ignored [the deputy's] command and walked away'; an officer who seriously burned a woman after detonating a 'flashbang' device in the bedroom where she was sleeping; an officer who deployed a dog against a suspect who 'claim[ed] that he surrendered by raising his hands in the air'; and an officer who shot an unarmed woman eight times after she threw a knife and glass at a police dog that was attacking her brother."

Bipartisan Middle Ground?

Supreme Court Justices across the ideological spectrum–including Justices Kennedy, Scalia, Thomas, and Sotomayer–have criticized the application of the qualified immunity doctrine. The question then arises: is it possible to retain qualified immunity when it clearly makes sense but to limit the doctrine when it merely provides cover for abuses like that in Jamison v. McClendon?

On the one hand, it seems hard to fault a police officer when he or she follows existing law and yet turns out to be wrong. For example, what if an officer executes a search based on a judicially-approved search warrant and a different judge later determines (as can happen in our judicial system) that the warrant did not contain a sufficient statement of probable cause or was invalid for some other reason? Should an officer become liable if he or she makes an arrest for a violation of a criminal statute that a court later determines was unconstitutional? In these cases, eliminating the defense of qualified immunity would seem to punish an officer who acted in good faith compliance with existing law.

On the other hand, the application of qualified immunity in cases of claimed excessive force in making an arrest, such as the Floyd and Blake cases, is often troublesome. Again, the officer will not have qualified immunity if the law is "clearly established" that what he did was illegal. Of course, the law is clearly established that it is unconstitutional to use excessive force. So you might think that officers will not have qualified immunity in excessive force cases. But, as it stands now, courts must assess the qualified immunity defense by looking not just at the general constitutional rule that it is illegal to use excessive force but rather at the specific facts of the case. In other words, the question trial judges have to answer is whether there are excessive force cases decided by appellate courts in which they found very similar police conduct to be illegal. Only if this factual similarity exists will the officer lose qualified immunity and become subject to a money judgment. Judge Reeves struggled with this rule in the Jamison case because no two cases are exactly the same, particularly when they involve violent police-citizen encounters. What the officers may have done illegally in the George Floyd case does not necessarily "clearly establish" that what happened in the Jacob Blake case was illegal. One can debate endlessly whether two cases are similar or different. For this reason, qualified immunity may be very difficult to deny in excessive force cases that are dependent on unique facts. That difficulty can lead to unjust results, as it may have in the Jamieson case.

In Conclusion

The main point here is that there seem to be some valid applications of qualified immunity and some invalid ones. Those calling for the complete elimination of qualified immunity for police officers go too far, especially when the officer acts in accordance with a judge's orders or existing law. Yet there may be a species of cases, perhaps those involving claims of excessive force, in which qualified immunity does not make sense. Even in these cases, the officer would not be liable unless the person suing the officer convinced a jury that the officer had actually violated the law. We must also consider the fact that there are other remedies for police misconduct such as the exclusionary rule (which prevents the government from using evidence at trial that the police obtain in violation of a suspect's rights), administrative discipline and, ultimately, criminal charges against the officer.

There is much room for debate and fine-tuning. Some of this debate will take place in courtrooms and among judges and Justices. Some of this debate can take place in legislatures. Here, as with so many other issues, there is a need for civil, bipartisan discussion to accomplish reform in view of contemporary events while still accommodating competing governmental and societal interests. I hope the readers of Divided We Fall will continue the conversation.

Viewpoint 5

> *"Democrats and younger Republicans back ending qualified immunity."*

The Majority Favors Giving Civilians the Power to Sue Police Officers for Misconduct

Pew Research Center

In the following viewpoint, the Pew Research Center uses polling data to argue that a majority of Americans believe that citizens should have the right to sue police officers for misconduct. In addition, Americans' ratings of police performance have declined from four years earlier. There is broad support for several reform proposals. Pew Research Center is a nonpartisan thinktank that conducts surveys and analyses on social issues and public opinion in the United States.

As you read, consider the following questions:

1. What percentage of Black adults say citizens should have the power to sue police?
2. What demographic factor is most significant regarding views of police funding?
3. What group is highest in their belief that the police are doing an excellent or good job of protecting people from crimes?

"Majority of Public Favors Giving Civilians the Power to Sue Police Officers for Misconduct," by Pew Research Center, July 9, 2020. Reprinted by permission.

With legislation to address racism and the use of excessive force by law enforcement stalled in Congress, there is broad public support in the United States for permitting citizens to sue police officers in order to hold them accountable for misconduct or using excessive force.

The legal doctrine of "qualified immunity" generally protects officers from being held personally liable in lawsuits unless they commit clear violations of law. A proposal to limit qualified immunity has emerged as a stumbling block in the congressional debate over policing.

Two-thirds of Americans (66%) say that civilians need to have the power to sue police officers to hold them accountable for misconduct and excessive use of force, even if that makes the officers' jobs more difficult. Just 32% say that, in order for police officers to do their jobs effectively, they need to be shielded from such lawsuits.

About eight-in-ten Black adults (86%) favor permitting citizens to sue police officers to hold them accountable for misconduct, as do 75% of Hispanic adults and 60% of white adults. There also are sizable partisan differences in views of qualified immunity, reflecting the divisions over the issue in Congress. A majority of Democrats and Democratic-leaning independents (84%) say citizens need the power to sue police officers for the use of excessive force and misconduct, compared with 45% of Republicans and Republican leaners.

The national survey, conducted June 16-22 among 4,708 adults using Pew Research Center's American Trends Panel, finds that the public's evaluations of police performance in several key areas have declined since the Center last explored attitudes among police officers and the public in 2016.

A 58% majority of Americans say police around the country do an excellent or good job of protecting people from crime, which is little changed from the share who said this four years ago (62%). However, there have been double-digit declines in the shares who say police forces do an excellent or good job of using the right amount of force for each situation (from 45% in 2016 to 35% today), treating racial and ethnic groups equally (47% to 34%) and holding officers accountable when misconduct occurs (44% to 31%).

The declines on all three measures have been comparable among Black and white adults. Democrats are far less positive about police performance than they were in 2016, while the change among Republicans has been less pronounced.

For example, just 10% of Democrats say police around the country do an excellent or good job in treating racial and ethnic groups equally, down from 27% in 2016. Nearly two-thirds of Republicans (64%) have a positive view of how police around the country do in treating racial and ethnic groups equally, which is a modest decline from four years ago (71%).

The survey finds little support for reducing spending on policing. Just 25% of Americans say spending on policing in their area should be decreased, with only 12% saying it should be decreased a lot; another 14% say it should be reduced a little.

A 73% majority say that spending on their local police should stay about the same as it is now (42%) or be increased from its current level (31%). While Black adults are more likely than whites to favor cuts in police budgets, fewer than half of Black adults (42%) say spending on policing in their areas should be reduced. That is double the share of white adults who favor cutting funding for their local police (21%).

There also are sizable age differences in views of funding for policing. Among both Black and white adults, those under age 50 are far more likely to support decreased funding for police in their areas than are those 50 and older.

The survey finds that Americans overwhelmingly favor requiring police to be trained in nonviolent alternatives to deadly force; 92% support this proposal, including 71% who strongly favor it.

Several other policing proposals draw broad support as well: 90% of the public favors a federal government database to track officers accused of misconduct. Three-quarters support giving civilian oversight boards the power to investigate and discipline officers accused of misconduct, and similar shares favor requiring officers to live in the places they police and outlawing police use of chokeholds or strangleholds.

While majorities of both parties and of Black, white and Hispanic adults favor each of these proposals, there are substantial differences in intensity of support on most of them. For example, while large shares of Black (87%) and white adults (71%) favor outlawing police use of chokeholds or strangleholds, nearly three-quarters of Black adults (74%) strongly favor this proposal, compared with fewer than half of white adults (44%).

Wide Racial, Partisan Gaps in Views of Police Performance

Americans are divided along partisan and racial lines in their evaluations of police. Across four measures of police performance, white adults are consistently more positive about the performance of police around the country than Black adults, and Republicans are much more positive than Democrats. While the partisan divide in positive evaluations of the police on most of these dimensions is nearly as wide among whites as it is overall, Black Democrats are more likely than their white counterparts to say that the police perform poorly.

Overall, a majority of Americans (58%) say that police around the country are doing an excellent or good job of protecting people from crimes—a view held by 78% of Republicans and Republican leaners but 43% of Democrats and Democratic leaners. Two-thirds of white adults (67%) say the police are doing a good or excellent job of protecting people, while just 28% of Black adults say the same. Half of Hispanic adults say police do an excellent or good job of protecting people.

There are racial and ethnic divides among Democrats in these views: While just 27% of Black Democrats say police do an excellent or good job protecting people from crime (and fully 72% say they do a poor job of this), about half of white Democrats (49%) and 42% of Hispanic Democrats say the same.

Public ratings of the police in three other areas—using the right amount of force for each situation, treating racial and ethnic groups equally and holding officers accountable when misconduct occurs—are considerably more negative, with more than six-in-ten Americans rating police performance in these domains as only fair or poor. Black Americans are especially likely to rate police negatively in each of these areas.

However, majorities of Republicans say that police are doing an excellent or good job of using the right amount of force for each situation (61%) and treating racial and ethnic groups equally (64%). About half of Republicans (51%) say that police around the country are doing an excellent or good job of holding officers accountable when misconduct occurs. Fewer than two-in-ten Democrats rate police positively in these areas.

While only about one in ten white Democrats and Black Democrats rate police performance in these three areas positively, Black Democrats are significantly more likely than white Democrats to say police are doing a poor job in each of these areas. For example, three-quarters of Black Democrats say that police are doing a poor job of using the right amount of force for each situation, compared with 46% of white Democrats who say this.

Hispanic Democrats are more positive in their evaluations of police performance in these domains than both white and Black Democrats; still, majorities rate police performance in these areas as only fair or poor.

Overall Ratings of the Police Have Declined Since 2016

Americans' ratings of police performance are lower than they were four years ago, and while substantial racial and partisan divides remain, these declines are largely seen among both white and Black adults.

The share of white Americans who say police are doing an excellent or good job of holding officers accountable for misconduct has fallen from half in 2016 to about one-third today (34%). The share of Black Americans who say this has also declined, from 21% to 12%.

The shares of white and Black adults who say police around the country are doing an excellent or good job of using the right amount of force have declined by identical amounts—10 percentage points each—since 2016. The shares saying police are doing an excellent or good job of treating racial and ethnic groups equally have also declined by identical amounts (11 points each).

There has been no significant change since 2016 in the shares of white and Black Americans saying that police are doing an excellent or good job of protecting people from crime.

While overall public evaluations of police performance have become more negative since 2016, declines among Democrats have generally been steeper than among Republicans.

Partisan gap on several evaluations of police performance wider than in 2016

Republicans today are about as likely to say that police around the country do an excellent or good job of protecting people from crime as they were four years ago (78% today vs. 74% in 2016). Among Democrats, about four-in-ten (43%) say that police do an excellent or good job of protecting people, down from about half (53%) in 2016.

Republicans are only slightly less likely to say police do an excellent or good job of treating racial and ethnic groups equally or using the right amount of force for each situation than they were previously, but Democrats' views on police performance in these areas have shifted downward more substantially. The share of Democrats who say police use appropriate force has decreased from 28% to 14%. And just one-in-ten Democrats now say that police do an excellent or good job of treating racial and ethnic groups equally, compared with about one-quarter (27%) who said this four years ago.

Republicans have changed the most in their views of police accountability. While nearly two-thirds (64%) said that police did an excellent or good job of holding officers accountable when misconduct occurs in 2016, only about half (51%) now say this. The share of Democrats who say police do an excellent or good job of holding officers accountable has decreased by a similar amount, from 27% to 13%.

Broad Public Support for Several Policing Reform Proposals

There is majority support among the public—and in both parties—for five policy proposals about policing included in the survey. However, there are still sizable partisan differences in these views.

Eight-in-ten or more Democrats either strongly or somewhat favor each of the five proposals, while there is more variation among Republicans. Even on policies where there is overwhelming bipartisan support—such as requiring police to be trained in nonviolent alternatives to deadly force, favored by nine-in-ten or more in both parties—Democrats are more likely than Republicans to strongly support such a policy (84% vs. 55%).

An overwhelming majority of Democrats (89%) say they favor giving civilian oversight boards power to investigate and discipline officers accused of misconduct, with 62% saying they strongly favor this. A narrower majority (58%) of Republicans say they either strongly or somewhat favor oversight boards (19% strongly favor). There is a similar pattern of opinion about making it a crime for police to use chokeholds or strangleholds (88% of Democrats and 57% of Republicans favor this).

Overwhelming majorities of both Republicans (85%) and Democrats (94%) favor creating a federal government database to track officers accused of misconduct. However, while about three-quarters of Democrats (77%) strongly favor this proposal, fewer than half of Republicans say the same (44%).

Large majorities of Republicans (91%) and Democrats (94%) also favor requiring police to be trained in nonviolent alternatives to deadly force. Among Democrats, 84% say they strongly favor this policy, while slightly more than half of Republicans (55%) say the same.

While majorities of white (71%), Black (82%) and Hispanic (81%) Americans favor giving civilian boards power to investigate and discipline officers, Black and Hispanic Americans are more likely than white Americans to favor this—and to do so strongly.

Nearly nine-in-ten Black adults (87%) favor making it a crime for police to use chokeholds or strangleholds, including 74% who do so strongly. This proposed policy is supported by 71% of white adults and 75% of Hispanic adults.

Seven-in-ten or more white (74%), Black (79%) and Hispanic (72%) adults say they favor requiring officers to live in the places they police, with Black Americans somewhat more likely than Hispanic and white Americans to strongly favor this.

And while the creation of a federal government database to track officers accused of misconduct is supported by wide majorities across racial and ethnic groups, Black adults are more likely than white adults to strongly favor this proposal.

Overwhelming majorities across racial and ethnic groups say they favor requiring police to be trained in nonviolent alternatives to deadly force, with at least seven-in-ten saying they strongly favor this.

Just a Quarter of the Public Says Spending on Police Should Be Decreased

About four-in-ten Americans (42%) say spending on policing in their area should stay about the same, while 31% say it should be increased and 25% say it should be decreased.

Support for decreasing spending on policing is higher among younger adults, Black adults, and Democrats and Democratic leaners, though even in these groups fewer than half say spending should be decreased.

Adults under 30 are much more likely than others to say that police spending should be decreased: 45% of those ages 18 to 29 say this, while 28% of those 30 to 49 and only 15% of those 50 and older say the same. Those over the age of 50 are more likely than younger Americans to say spending should be increased (37% say this, compared with 29% of 30- to 49-year-olds and 22% of those under 30).

About four-in-ten Black adults (42%) say spending on police in their area should decrease, including 22% who say spending should be decreased a lot. One-third of Black adults say spending should stay the same, while 22% say it should be increased.

In contrast, about two-in-ten white adults (21%) and a similar share of Hispanic adults (24%) say police spending in their area should be decreased, while larger shares in both groups (33% and 37%, respectively) say spending should be increased.

Among Democrats and Democratic-leaning independents, 41% say spending on the police should be decreased, while just 8% of Republicans say the same. By comparison, 45% of Republicans and just 19% of Democrats that spending on the police should be increased (46% of Republicans and 38% of Democrats say spending should stay the same).

Among Democrats there are sizable age and ideological differences on this question.

White and Black Democrats are nearly equally likely to say that spending should be decreased (43% and 42% respectively); Hispanic Democrats are somewhat less likely to say this (32%). And while 34% of Hispanic Democrats say funding should be increased, that compares with 23% of Black Democrats and just 14% of white Democrats.

Younger Democrats are far more likely to say that spending on the police should be decreased. Similar majorities of white (57%) and Black (53%) Democrats under the age of 50 say that spending should be decreased, with nearly a third saying it should be decreased a lot (30% and 32%, respectively). By comparison, only about three-in-ten white and Black Democrats ages 50 and older (28% and 29%, respectively) say police spending should be decreased.

Liberal Democrats are much more likely to say that police spending should be decreased than conservative and moderate Democrats (57% vs. 27%). Democrats who say they are "very" liberal are particularly likely to hold this view—68% say funding for police should be decreased, compared with 52% among those who say they are liberal (but not very liberal).

Democrats and Younger Republicans Back Ending Qualified Immunity

Among Republicans, there are sizable divides by age when it comes to whether civilians should be able to sue the police: 61% of Republicans ages 18 to 29 say civilians need to have the power to sue police officers in order to hold them accountable, compared with about half of those 30 to 64 (47%) and just 31% of those 65 and older.

While at least three-quarters of Democrats in all age groups say that civilians should be able to sue the police, younger Democrats are more likely to say this: 87% of Democrats ages 18 to 29 say civilians need the power to sue the police, while slightly fewer Democrats 65 and older say the same (79%).

Eight-in-ten or more white (84%), Black (89%) and Hispanic (82%) Democrats say that civilians should have the power to sue police. White Democrats are much more likely than white Republicans to say this (84% vs. 43%).

Periodical and Internet Sources Bibliography

The following articles have been selected to supplement the diverse views presented in this chapter.

Ariane de Vogue, "Supreme Court sides with police officers in two qualified immunity cases," CNN, October 18, 2021. https://www.cnn.com/2021/10/18/politics/qualified-immunity-supreme-court/index.html

Mike Killer, "We must end 'qualified immunity' for police. It might save the next George Floyd," The Guardian, April 20, 2021. https://www.theguardian.com/commentisfree/2021/apr/20/george-floyd-derek-chauvin-killer-mike-police

Kimberly Kindy, "Dozens of states have tried to end qualified immunity. Police officers and unions helped beat nearly every bill.," The Washington Post, October 7, 2021. https://www.washingtonpost.com/politics/qualified-immunity-police-lobbying-state-legislatures/2021/10/06/60e546bc-0cdf-11ec-aea1-42a8138f132a_story.html

Dan King, "Some States Moving on 'Qualified Immunity' Reform," The Bulwark, March 30, 2021. https://www.thebulwark.com/some-states-moving-on-qualified-immunity-reform/

Nancy La Vigne, Marc Levin, "Five myths about qualified immunity," The Washington Post, May 27, 2021.https://www.washingtonpost.com/outlook/five-myths/five-myths-about-qualified-immunity/2021/05/27/db829e38-bcbc-11eb-9c90-731aff7d9a0d_story.html

Marianne Levine, Nicholas Wu, "Lawmakers scrap qualified immunity deal in police reform talks," Politico, August 17, 2021. https://www.politico.com/news/2021/08/17/lawmakers-immunity-police-reform-talks-505671

Eric Schnurer, "Congress Is Going to Have to Repeal Qualified Immunity," The Atlantic, June 17, 2020. https://www.theatlantic.com/ideas/archive/2020/06/congress-going-have-repeal-qualified-immunity/613123/

Jay Schweikert, "Qualified Immunity: A Legal, Practical, and Moral Failure," The Cato Institute, September 14, 2020. https://www.cato.org/policy-analysis/qualified-immunity-legal-practical-moral-failure

Seth W. Stoughton, Jeffrey J., Noble Geoffrey P., Alpert, "How to Actually Fix America's Police," The Atlantic, June 3, 2020. https://www.theatlantic.com/ideas/archive/2020/06/how-actually-fix-americas-police/612520/

Emma Tucker, "States tackling 'qualified immunity' for police as Congress squabbles over the issue," CNN, April 23, 2021. https://www.cnn.com/2021/04/23/politics/qualified-immunity-police-reform/index.html

OPPOSING VIEWPOINTS® SERIES

Chapter 4

Is "Defund the Police" an Effective Strategy for Police Reform?

Chapter Preface

Support for police reform in the United States surged following the murder of George Floyd by a police officer in Minneapolis in 2020. Public demonstrations around the country throughout the summer of 2020 showed a reinvigorated movement with new and aggressive policy proposals to limit police violence and re-orient the focus of public safety and law enforcement in the United States. The most prominent and widely debated of these proposals came to be known as "Defund the Police" (the phrase would also become shorthand for pro-reform activist groups on the political Left).

The basic concept behind Defund the Police is not new. The idea is that many of the elements involved in preserving public safety and order could be accomplished more directly—and with much less collateral damage—by social workers and mental health professionals than by today's militarized police forces. In the aftermath of George Floyd's murder by police officers, many activists framed the proposal as a matter of moral necessity in light of the clearly outrageous behavior of Floyd's killers. The pro-reform movement embraced the moment as the final straw following years of advocacy and public awareness campaigns they felt had yielded little in the way of concrete results.

But the concept of defunding the police ran into immediate resistance from law enforcement officers, many of whom had offered immediate and public acknowledgment of the egregious nature of the conduct by officers involved in George Floyd's murder. Over the course of 2020—a presidential election year that had also seen the introduction of the COVID-19 pandemic—it became clear that political support for the Defund the Police movement was extremely limited, and the opposition was formidable.

Nonetheless, pro-reform activists on the left have continued to embrace the overall concept and to promote softer versions of the original proposals as part of legislative and policy reform efforts. It seems clear that Defund the Police (as both an idea and a movement) will continue to play a role in the conversation about police reform in America.

VIEWPOINT 1

> *"Police must be the last resort, used only when necessary to protect the public from harm."*

Correcting Misconceptions About "Defund the Police"

Howard Henderson and Ben Yisrael

In the following viewpoint Howard Henderson and Ben Yisrael rebut a number of arguments that have been advanced by critics of the Defund the Police movement. At several points, they introduce research to suggest that the benefits of a police-first public safety philosophy are much less clear than we might think. Howard Henderson is the Founding Director of the Center for Justice Research, a Nonresident Senior Fellow at the Brookings Institution, and a professor at Texas Southern University. Ben Yisrael is a community advocate with decades of experience managing grassroots political organizations and a Postdoctoral Policy Fellow at the Center for Justice Research.

"7 myths About 'Defunding the Police' Debunked," by Howard Henderson and Ben Yisrael, The Brookings Institution, May 19, 2021. Reprinted by permission.

As you read, consider the following questions:

1. According to the authors, what is the difference between defunding the police and abolishing the police?
2. What are some of the costs that the authors associate with the failure to implement effective police reforms in the United States?
3. Why do the authors believe that the police are less effective at reducing violence than we might think?

Policing in the U.S. is a highly politicized issue with a history intertwined with racial and class-based struggle. During the summer of 2020, no issue was debated more than the subject of defunding the police. The phrase "defund the police" (DTP) became a rallying cry for the progressive left. Yet, while the movement gained considerable news coverage, the two major political parties, media, and major presidential candidates labeled defunding the police as an unrealistic demand.

This mischaracterization of the movement is not based on fact but rather fear. In this article, we address seven common myths associated with the campaign with the goal to demonstrate that while some have labeled it a radical movement, the DTP philosophy is based on well-researched, evidence-based positions.

Myth #1: Defund Means Abolish

One of the most misleading critiques of the movement is instigating defund means abolish. Opposers claim the movement undermines public safety through its efforts to end policing. The truth: the movement seeks to demilitarize police departments and reallocate funding to trained mental health workers and social workers to reduce unnecessary violent encounters between police and citizens. At least 13 cities in the United States have currently engaged in policy programs to defund the police.

Myth #2: Defunding Will Lead to Disorder

Another misconception is that police forces are what maintains order. However, studies have found that the best tools to establish peaceful societies are equity in education and infrastructure. Indeed, research shows that lack of education and illiteracy are some of the most significant predictors of future prison populations.

Myth #3: Police Protect the Public From Violence

Critics of the police movement assert that we need heavily funded and armed police forces to protect the public from violent criminal elements. However, there isn't sufficient data to support that position. In fact, research has found that the police don't have a notoriously efficient track record of solving violent crime. Further, what the research does show is that 70% of robberies, 66% of rapes, 47% of aggravated assaults, and 38% of murders go unsolved each year.

Myth #4: Community Programs Won't Work

While much of the available research contradicts the narrative that policing is essential to eliminating crime, substantial evidence shows that investing, developing, and supporting education and economic programs do, in fact, lead to less offenses and create more social harmony. Education has long been viewed as the great equalizer. Data supports the position that individuals that receive a quality education are less likely to become involved in the criminal justice system.

Myth #5: Most Police Work is Focused on Crime Prevention

There is minimal evidence that police surveillance results in reduced crime or prevents crime. For instance, research showed 90% of the people that were stopped in the NYPD's controversial stop and frisk program were not committing any crime. While it is true that police do apprehend individuals that violate the law, this is one of several components of their responsibilities.

Myth #6: Police Officers Do Not Need College Degrees

Research shows police officers that have at least two years of a college education are less likely to have misconduct complaints and less likely to use force to gain compliance. And, officers with only high school diplomas account for 75% of disciplinary problems. The evidence shows reform efforts should not ignore the application pool crisis and law enforcement departments should instill more robust higher education standards.

Myth #7: Defunding the Police is a Knee-Jerk Reaction with No Research

Some opponents of cutting police budgets view the movement as an emotional response to police misconduct rather than a well-thought-out campaign. However, a study with 60 years of data indicates that increases in spending do not reduce crime. Which begs the question, how is 60 years of a failed objective any better? Yes, the movement gained attention because of tragic events in 2020, but the evidence supporting the movement is based on hard data and proven methods.

Police reform is long overdue, and we have had thousands of opportunities to make the appropriate changes. In 2020, the murder of George Floyd garnered national attention that has caused many to take a long, hard look at our democratic systems, cultural identities, and the necessary steps towards equal protection. We do know that more traditional policing is not the answer.

No matter what we choose to call it, defund the police, a reallocation of funding, or a total reimagination, research supports a public health approach to policing. If we are effective, funding public health approaches will reduce the reliance on law-and-order policing, save lives and reverse the longstanding slide in the wrong direction. Police must be the last resort, used only when necessary to protect the public from harm. Until then, municipalities will need to prepare for the impact of increased police accountability and transparency. Ultimately the rising costs associated with police misconduct will force police reform, a cost that would have been much cheaper had we listened to those groups most impacted by aggressive policing. To see real change in our society, policymakers must remove the barriers and fund necessary programming. We need not raise taxes. We simply need to be smart and follow the science.

Viewpoint 2

> *"Police officers are not as successful as people think at solving violent crime."*

Why "Defund the Police" Makes Sense as a Strategy and a Policy Plan

Rashawn Ray

In the following viewpoint Rashawn Ray surveys the landscape of research on police reform concepts embraced by members of the Defund the Police movement. He presents data and theory in support of many of the initiatives, but he also suggests that it would be more accurate to discuss the policies in terms of reallocating public safety funds, as opposed to defunding law enforcement. Rashawn Ray is a Senior Fellow at The Brookings Institution and Executive Director of the Lab for Applied Social Science Research (LASSR) at the University of Maryland, where he also serves as Professor of Sociology.

As you read, consider the following questions:

1. Why does the author believe that police officers' skill set is often poorly aligned with the work they do on a day-to-day basis?
2. Why does the author propose that increases in education funding go hand-in-hand with the Defund the Police concept?

"What Does 'Defund the Police' Mean and Does It Have Merit?" by Rashawn Ray, The Brookings Institution, June 19, 2020. Reprinted by permission.

3. How much of a police officer's job involves the direct defense of public safety?

George Floyd's death has galvanized much of America to move the needle toward police reform ideas—such as defunding police—that were previously viewed as radical.

"Defund the police" means reallocating or redirecting funding away from the police department to other government agencies funded by the local municipality. That's it. It's that simple. Defund does not mean abolish policing. And, even some who say abolish, do not necessarily mean to do away with law enforcement altogether. Rather, they want to see the rotten trees of policing chopped down and fresh roots replanted anew. Camden, New Jersey, is a good example. Nearly a decade ago, Camden disbanded (abolished) its police force and dissolved the local police union. This approach seems to be what Minneapolis will do in some form, though the nuances are important.

Different from abolishing and starting anew, defunding police highlights fiscal responsibility, advocates for a market-driven approach to taxpayer money, and has some potential benefits that will reduce police violence and crime. Below, I outline some of the main arguments for defunding the police.

Calls for Service

Data show that 9 out of 10 calls for service are for nonviolent encounters. Now, this does not mean that an incident will not turn violent, but police at times contribute to the escalation of violent force. Police officers' skillset and training are often out of sync with the social interactions that they have. Police officers are mostly trained in use-of-force tactics and worst-case scenarios to reduce potential threats. However, most of their interactions with civilians start with a conversation.

Advocates for the defund movement like Phillip McHarris and Thenjiwe McHarris argue that shifting funding to social services that can improve things such as mental health, addiction, and homelessness is a better use of taxpayer money. This approach further enhances the push to decriminalize and destigmatize people with mental health conditions and addiction problems. Ever since the overcriminalization of people addicted to crack cocaine in the 1990s, some scholars, practitioners, and policymakers have said that this shift is long overdue.

Additionally, the research I have conducted with hundreds of police officers show that they respond to everything from potholes in the street to cats stuck up a tree. Police officers are also increasingly asked to complete paperwork and online forms. Obviously, documentation is important and desperately needed. The overwhelmingly blank report in the killing of Breonna Taylor in Louisville that listed her injuries as "none" highlights the importance of documentation. It could be argued, however, that reducing officer workload would increase the likelihood of solving violent crimes. Police officers are overworked and overstressed. Focusing on menial tasks throughout the day is inefficient and a waste of taxpayer money. Other government actors should be responsible for these and receive adequate funding for doing them.

Homicide Clearance Rate

Police officers are not as successful as people think at solving violent crime. My Brookings colleagues Andre Perry, David Harshbarger, Carl Romer, and Kristian Thymianos argue that "the failure to prosecute murderous police typifies a bad overall track record with solving violent crimes: Approximately 38% of murders, 66% of rapes, 70% of robberies, and 47% of aggravated assaults go uncleared every year." Maybe in baseball or basketball these rates make a player an all-star, but the public expects police officers to be more successful at solving violent crime.

More importantly, police stops relative to charges and convictions are relatively low. To show how egregious this is, a study of the NYPD stop-and-frisk program found that well over 90% of people stopped by the police were not committing any crime and did not have any contraband or weapons on them. Overwhelmingly, the people stopped were Black and Latino, and physical force was used half the time. Interestingly, police were more successful at identifying criminality for whites versus Blacks. This is because officers use suspicious behavior when interacting with whites and use skin tone as the metric of suspicion when interacting with Black people. More police on the streets may be used to control the movement of Black bodies rather than solving crime. This is why the New York State Supreme Court ruled stop-and-frisk as unconstitutional. No-knock warrants and chokeholds should follow this pattern.

Education and Work Infrastructure

One consistent finding in the social science literature is that if we really want to reduce crime, education equity and the establishment of a work infrastructure is the best approach. A study using 60 years of data found that an increase in funding for police did not significantly relate to a decrease in crime. Throwing more police on the street to solve a structural problem is one of the reasons why people are protesting in the streets. Defunding police—reallocating funding away from police departments to other sectors of government—may be more beneficial for reducing crime and police violence.

What Defunding Looks Like

In recent weeks, some large municipalities with a history of police brutality have reallocated funds in line with the defund police movement. Los Angeles will have at least $100 million reallocated away from LAPD to programs for minority communities. San Francisco Mayor London Breed said that she will work with community groups to reprioritize funding. Baltimore City Council voted to reallocate $22 million away from the police department's fiscal budget for 2021, which is typically over $500 million. The city council plans to redirect the funding to recreational centers, trauma centers, and forgivable loans for Black-owned businesses.

Prince George's County, Maryland, aims to reallocate $20 million away from a new training facility for its police department (though the money will not come out of the police department's budget) and to remove student resource officers from schools. Other areas, such as Minneapolis, have advocated for removing police officers from schools as well.

Altogether, it is clear that municipalities across the U.S. are making changes in line with the defund police movement. So, while the word "reallocate" may be a more palatable, digestible word on the House floor or at a city council meeting, "defund" surely gets more attention on a protest sign. And more importantly, it seems to be having an impact.

Viewpoint 3

> *"'Defund the police' is something of a Rorschach inkblot test—people bring their own interpretations to the phrase."*

A Deeper Look at the Concept Behind "Defund the Police"

Clark Merrefield

In the following excerpted viewpoint Clark Merrefield examines a number of different perspectives on the "Defund the Police" movement and the policy concepts that have been associated with the movement. He interviews a number of researchers, law enforcement experts, and community leaders, and applies a more nuanced analysis than some of the more ideological defenses and criticisms of the movement that have attracted attention in the media over the past several years. Clark Merrefield is Senior Editor for Economics at Journalist's Resource, a publication under Harvard University's Kennedy School of Government. He was previously a reporter at Newsweek and The Daily Beast.

As you read, consider the following questions:

1. What impact did the shuttering of mental institutions in the 1970s have on law enforcement work in the United States?

2. What can we learn from the results of Camden, New Jersey, disbanding its police force in 2013?
3. What are some of the differences between the "guardian" model and the "warrior" model of how police should operate in the community?

Last June, video of white Minneapolis police officer Derek Chauvin killing George Floyd, a Black man, went viral on social media. Uprisings took hold across hundreds of U.S. cities, and activist calls to "defund the police" went mainstream.

For some, "defund the police" is a movement, a stepping stone toward abolishing police departments entirely.

For others, the idea of defunding the police is limited to simply restricting money for military-style equipment.

For many, the definition lies in the middle—there should be police, but their role in communities should be limited to crime prevention. The idea goes that service agencies other than police could and should respond to non-violent calls related to mental health, housing and other issues. Berkeley, California has even moved to create a separate department to handle routine traffic violations.

Here, we explore what "defund the police" means to leading criminologists, community organizers and legal scholars; recent academic research on whether more police presence reduces crime; and what the future of policing in America might look like.

The National Conversation on 'Defund' Is Ongoing

CBS Evening News anchor Norah O'Donnell asked Joe Biden whether he supported defunding the police on June 9, 2020.

"No, I don't support defunding the police," the then-presidential candidate said. "I support conditioning federal aid to police based on whether or not they meet certain basic standards of decency and honorableness and, in fact, are able to demonstrate they can protect the community and everybody in the community."

Nearly two dozen cities have since taken steps to reduce police funding or redirect funds toward other services—though the 50 largest U.S. cities slightly increased their law enforcement spending as a percentage of their combined 2021 budgets.

As some cities recalibrate police spending, "defund the police" remains relevant, and contentious, in the national conversation.

Earlier this week on "Fox News Sunday," host Chris Wallace asked U.S. Rep. Jim Banks of Indiana why he and other Republicans voted against a COVID-19 relief package that directed billions toward community programs and policing, including hiring more officers.

Wallace asked, "Can't you make the argument that it's you and Republicans who are defunding the police?"

Banks replied, "Not at all, Chris." After some back-and-forth with Wallace, Banks pivoted to political rivals:

"When Rep. [Ilhan] Omar says that policing is rooted in evil and [House Speaker] Nancy Pelosi compares police officers to Nazi storm troopers, it makes it very difficult for police departments around the country to recruit people to become police officers."

In July 2020, in response to President Donald Trump sending camouflaged and heavily armed federal law enforcement to Portland, Oregon, to arrest protesters and protect federal property, Pelosi tweeted, "Unidentified storm troopers. Unmarked cars. Kidnapping protesters and causing severe injuries in response to graffiti."

It's unclear whether Omar has described a specific law enforcement department or police generally as "evil."

But she has called the Minneapolis Police Department a "cancer" and "rotten to the root."

Different Interpretations of 'Defund'

"Defund the police" is something of a Rorschach inkblot test—people bring their own interpretations to the phrase.

"'Defund the police' means reallocating or redirecting funding away from the police department to other government agencies

A Terrible Idea That Risks Safety

As the retired commander of the internal affairs unit for an agency of nearly 1,000 FDLE-certified correctional officers, I clearly recognize the enormity of the recent events in Minneapolis as well as the outrage and review of the reprehensible behavior of the officers involved. One of the end results in this sad and ugly event has some communities discussing the possibility of defunding their police agencies. Seriously?

Not only is the idea itself insane, it's hard to imagine it would get any traction in any community, even one where a bad cop killed a man who was cuffed behind his back begging for his life. The behavior was despicable and the officer should be and will be held accountable.

Some of these remedies being offered are not actually remedies to anything. They are merely comfort food for those with an appetite for the spotlight. Some days it almost seems as if people, and companies, are competing with each other to see who can make the next exaggerated move that will grab a headline. We would be better served if everyone would slow down a little bit and take a meaningful, realistic approach to addressing inequities wherever they may exist.

There is no doubt we live in a world of societal differences, with biases from all sides. And it is laudable that so many people and companies are now seeking to address these issues. At the same time, it's also unfortunate that it takes such an event to create a desire for everyone to take action and review our societal landscape.

As the leader of my investigative unit, I oversaw dozens of cases each year and reviewed each and every one prior to disposition. Most of these cases involved complaints related to officer off-duty behavior. However, there were occasional complaints as to force used and racial misconduct and there were occasions where officers were fired, both white and black.

Whether improvements can be made in law enforcement agencies is a question that will always be answered with one word: Yes. However, the defunding of an agency is counterproductive to the well-being and safety of everyone.

Everyone should take a deep breath and move forward one meaningful step at a time and make changes that actually make a difference. We need to stop the insanity.

"Defunding Police: A Terrible Idea That Risks Safety," by Dennis Warren, The Orlando Sentinel, June 18, 2020.

funded by the local municipality," writes University of Maryland sociologist Rashawn Ray in a June 2020 Brookings Institution blog post. "That's it. It's that simple."

Around the same time as Ray's writing, activist and educator Mariame Kaba wrote a New York Times opinion essay titled, "Yes, we mean literally abolish the police."

"We are not abandoning our communities to violence," Kaba writes. "We don't want to just close police departments. We want to make them obsolete."

Criminologist Brooklynn Hitchens, an incoming assistant professor at the University of Maryland, put it like this: "I do feel police are deeply corrupt and troubled and I don't know how to work within a system that is that corrupt," she says. "But, at its core, 'defund' the police is about reallocation of funds to more social service-based agencies, whether it's housing or mental health."

Peter Moskos, a criminologist at the John Jay College of Criminal Justice, questions why money for expanding social services should come from police coffers.

"I'm all for funding mental health issues and homeless issues, but the idea that it has to come from the 5% of city budgets that goes to law enforcement is absurd," he says.

Seth Stoughton, an associate professor of law at the University of South Carolina, sees "defund" as shorthand for more social service investment, as well as reexamining what law enforcement means in America.

"Homelessness, poverty, substance abuse—we've criminalized a range of human behaviors and we've relied on the police to be the social service agency not just of first resort, but sometimes our only social service agency that deals with these issues," he says. "So what I think when I hear 'defund the police' tends to be, 'Reduce the need for police to respond to some of these social issues by investing in a more robust overarching social service infrastructure.'"

[…]

A Range of Policing Futures

Law professors Stephen Rushin and Roger Michalski, writing in the Florida Law Review in 2020, suggest that widespread defunding of police departments "could increase crime rates, hamper efforts to control officer misconduct, and reduce officer safety."

Rushin and Michalski take "defund" at face value, meaning police budget cuts. Instead of defunding police departments, they propose states redistribute policing funds equitably to localities, including money for officer training and accountability efforts.

"Just as some state legislatures have passed revenue-sharing initiatives designed to equalize the availability of public goods such as education, so, too, should states act to equalize the funding of local police departments according to need," they write.

In contrast to a redistributive funding framework, Ohio State University law professor Amna Akbar argues in a December 2020 California Law Review article that scholars need to take seriously activist calls for abolishing the police. Akbar writes:

> Abolitionist demands like "defund the police" remind us that if we are interested in building a more just world, we cannot wage our battles simply on the terrain of rights, litigation, rule of law, or administrative innovation. We must consider the historical, material, and ideological dimensions of our demands and our strategies. We must examine where we invest money and what kind of infrastructure we build for collective life. We must investigate the ideas that motivate and justify things as they are. We must appraise who has what resources, for what end, and why. We have to understand how such profound inequity came to be, why it persists, and what needs to be redressed to create the equitable society we aspire to but have not yet realized. We have to ask: If police and prisons are the stuff of structural violence, what are the elements of structural flourishing, and what are the strategies to build them?

Some prominent law enforcement professionals have indicated an openness for shifting police responsibilities away from non-criminal situations.

"The police would be very happy to get rid of responsibilities which were forced upon them in the first place," former New York City police commissioner and former Los Angeles police chief Bill Bratton told The Crime Report earlier this month. "We created the homeless problem when we closed down mental institutions back in the 1970s. But there was no [follow-up] funding for the homeless."

Bratton added: "If you take that responsibility entirely away from the police—who work 24 hours a day—you're going to have to create a huge budget in other agencies needed to staff these functions 24 hours a day. I would suggest, you know, as we go forward with these efforts, we're going to find the police are like weaving a garment, that we are going to be a central thread in that garment, no matter who they give the responsibility to."

University of Arkansas criminologist Jordan Blair Woods, in a forthcoming Stanford Law Review article, suggests redirecting another core function away from police: traffic enforcement.

"A major obstacle to achieving structural police reform in this important moment for policing is the conventional wisdom that a robust police force is needed to enforce traffic laws," Woods writes. "'This obstacle is especially problematic given that traffic policing is a persistent source of race- and class-based injustice."

A handful of cities in recent years have proposed divesting traffic stops from policing. Last July, lawmakers in Berkeley approved a new traffic enforcement department separate from the police department.

Princeton University sociologist Patrick Sharkey in a June 2020 Washington Post essay recalled traveling to Western Australia in 2017 to observe the work of the Nyoongar Patrol, a government-funded patrol made up of community members:

> I watched them break up a fight between two young people before the police were called. At the end of the night, I saw them make calls to find a safe place to sleep for a woman who was worried that she would be at risk if she went home. I observed from the periphery, and I was still exhausted by the end of the shift. It

> is hard, stressful work to spend time in public spaces, making sure everyone feels safe. But it works better if those taking on this task are motivated by genuine concern for their neighbors.

[…]

The Case of Camden, New Jersey

Police budgets sometimes shrink after recessions, as jobs disappear, tax dollars dwindle and federal funding is redirected. The Marshall Project reported in June 2020 that community trust eroded and there were more complaints about officer use of force when police budgets were cut in Memphis and Chicago after the Great Recession.

But, as The Marshall Project notes, there is at least one fundamental difference between recessionary reductions and the "defund" discussion. Local police budget cuts due to waning financial resources seek the survival of the force. Calls to defund the police over the past year are aimed at rethinking policing entirely.

Camden, New Jersey, often comes up as an example of a city that reframed its approach to policing and reduced crime. It also spent more to do so.

Camden disbanded its police force in 2013 after one of the city's most violent years on record. Camden County took over and in May 2013 formed a new department, the Camden County Police Department, to patrol the city.

CCPD instituted community-based policing tactics along with new technology, such as a video observation platform covering a six-block radius.

Overall crime per 100,000 Camdenites decreased by more than half from 2012 to 2020, according to CCPD data, while the number of shooting homicides fell by 68%.

"Camden got more money," Moskos says. "More money is not a panacea, but you're not going to get better for less money. That's my issue with 'defund.' It makes policing worse. It is that simple. The people who generally want to abolish police think police don't prevent crime."

Research published in late 2019 in Preventive Medicine Reports also associates the new policing tactics in Camden with lower rates of gunshot patients at a major regional trauma center. On average, there were 34 gunshot patients treated every three months before the policing changes, and 26 quarterly gunshot patients afterward.

"The ways in which police there actively engaged with the community worked," says Hitchens. "Crime did go down in the city. But Camden is still a very poor and distressed community. So the root causes that increase crime are still there."

She adds: "As a country, we are very punitive. But if you get at the root causes of crime—poverty, poor schools, poor housing—attacking it from that angle has been demonstrated time and time again as an effective way to reduce crime."

Warrior or Guardian?

One way for communities and police departments to rethink policing in America is to pursue a cultural shift of what it means to be an officer on patrol.

Stoughton, the University of South Carolina law professor, has for years advocated that police should think of themselves first as guardians, not as warriors. He wrote "Principled Policing: Warrior Cops and Guardian Officers," published in October 2016 in the Wake Forest Law Review.

This philosophical shift is perhaps most critical for beat cops, says Stoughton, because beat cops often represent the primary interaction community members have with law enforcement.

Stoughton himself served as a beat cop in Tallahassee for five years in the early 2000s.

It's about an individual officer's default mindset, Stoughton explains. Are they a warrior? Or a guardian?

Here's how he puts it:

"What is their job supposed to be—are they primarily there to kick ass and take names? Or to pull people over and get a bunch of citations written? Or, are they there to improve quality of life? Are they there to advance public safety? In other words, are they there to identify and deal with an enemy, or are they there in service to the community?"

There are two key elements to Stoughton's questions. The first is that an officer being a warrior or a guardian is not an either-or proposition—it's not a dichotomy. An officer will have to be a warrior sometimes—in an active shooter situation, for example—while reverting to a guardian mindset day-to-day. Many officers spend the bulk of their time responding to non-criminal calls and traffic violations.

"The point is that officers need to be more than just warriors," Stoughton says. "If that's all an officer is capable of, they aren't going to be a very good officer. Being a warrior is a small part of what officers need to bring to the job. The overarching part of what they need to bring to the job is this approach of guardianship—a service-oriented mentality."

Recent preliminary research suggests the race and ethnicity of patrol officers could make a difference as to whether they are open to thinking of themselves first as guardians. An online, non-representative pilot survey of 882 patrol officers from around the country, published in January 2021 in the Journal of Police and Criminal Psychology, finds officers overall receptive to both the guardian and warrior mindset, with Hispanic officers "more supportive of this hybrid style of policing than White officers."

(Response rates were too low for officers of other races and ethnicities to draw insight on whether they would be open to a guardian-first policing framework.)

The metaphor of guardian versus warrior isn't just academic—it's practical too, Stoughton says. Day-to-day policing can be mundane, but situations can change quickly.

"We use metaphor to communicate values," Stoughton says. "When you don't have clear guidance as to how to make a decision in a particular circumstance, you fall back on your values and principles."

Stoughton learned the guardian mentality firsthand while patrolling Tallahassee, even if the word "guardian" wasn't used at the time, and even if he didn't yet understand it.

He particularly recalls an arrest warrant issued one evening around 11 p.m. Stoughton's lieutenant told officers to wait to execute the warrant—it wouldn't be a good look for the department to arrest a community member in the middle of the night.

"I remember thinking at the time, 'That's bullshit. This is a legal process. We should be allowed to do it,'" Stoughton says. "In retrospect, I think the lieutenant was exactly right. We don't want to give the impression that we exist to knock down people's doors late at night and tear them away from their families."

He adds: "When and how we execute an arrest is as important as the fact of doing it."

Viewpoint 4

> *"More Americans are now joining the call to reevaluate the role of law enforcement and to shift some police responsibilities to professionals outside the justice system."*

The Value and Promise of Community-Based Approaches to Public Safety

Betsy Pearl

In this excerpted viewpoint Betsy Pearl looks at the landscape of alternative public safety concepts that have been proposed and studied by researchers and activists interested in macro-level law enforcement reform. She focuses particularly on the Office of Neighborhood Safety (ONS) model, which has been implemented in Richmond, California, and a handful of other municipalities. Pearl argues that Americans have overestimated the effectiveness of traditional police work from a public safety standpoint and that other approaches could offer better results, in some cases with less funding. Betsy Pearl was a policy advisor in the Department of Justice Office of Justice Programs. She currently serves as Associate Director for Criminal Justice Reform at the Center for American Progress.

"Beyond Policing: Investing in Offices of Neighborhood Safety," by Betsy Pearl, Center for American Progress, October 15, 2020. Reprinted by permission.

As you read, consider the following questions:

1. According to the viewpoint, what are some of the consequences of relying on the police for services other than the prevention of violent crime?
2. What are some of the differences between the Office of Neighborhood Safety (ONS) model and traditional policing?
3. Why does the author believe that the ONS public safety model could endure budget cutbacks more effectively than the police model?

In recent years, a series of high-profile cases of police violence—from Michael Brown, Tamir Rice and Eric Garner to George Floyd, Breonna Taylor, and Jacob Blake—has brought to the national consciousness concerns that have been prevalent among many activists, researchers, and policymakers: What should we expect of the police? Who is responsible for public safety? And what does it mean to invest in safety beyond policing?

The traditional understanding of public safety in the United States has revolved almost exclusively around policing, which is demonstrated by the size of the footprint of police agencies and their corresponding budgets. For example, the number of police officers nationwide has grown by 36 percent in two decades—from less than 700,000 officers in 1990 to more than 950,000 in 2012. As the size of American police forces grew, so too did their role in the community. "Efforts to address underlying community problems through social investment took a backseat [to] policing strategies," noted political scientists Joe Soss and Vesla Weaver. The duties of the modern police force now extend well beyond enforcing the law, to include tasks from treating overdoses and de-escalating behavioral health crises to addressing homelessness and responding to disciplinary concerns in schools. Law enforcement now spends only a fraction of their time responding to issues of violence: American police officers make more than 10 million arrests each year, less than 5 percent of which are for serious violent crimes.

The impact of police force expansion on community safety is debatable at best. While determining the cause of crime rate fluctuations is a notoriously difficult task, an analysis from the Brennan Center for Justice finds that the increase in officers had only a modest effect on crime rates in the 1990s, accounting for between 0 percent and 10 percent of the total crime reduction. Police growth continued between 2000 and 2012, with no discernible effect on crime rates. Instead, societal factors, such as growth in income, likely played a more important part in reducing crime rates during the 1990s and 2000s. Sociologist Patrick Sharkey has also analyzed factors contributing to crime reductions between 1990 and 2012, concluding that community-based organizations likely played a "substantial role in explaining the decline in violence" during this time period. In a city of 100,000 people, every new nonprofit focused on neighborhood safety and wellness was associated with an estimated 1 percent reduction in violent crime and homicide.

The problem with overreliance on law enforcement goes beyond its questionable impact on crime rates, however. When officers are dispatched in response to a wide range of concerns, more and more civilians become unnecessarily ensnared in the justice system. In 2016, Americans were arrested 2.18 million times for alcohol misuse, liquor law violations, and drug-related charges—more than four times the total number of arrests for all serious violent crimes combined. In particular, overreliance on law enforcement has created profound consequences for Black communities, who have long been subjected to overpolicing and aggressive enforcement tactics. Any brush with the criminal justice system, however minor, can have permanent consequences. Even arrests that don't result in a conviction come with a criminal record—and with it, a lifetime of barriers to education, employment, housing, and other basic building blocks of a healthy life. Too often, interactions with the police can prove fatal. Police violence is a leading cause of death for Black men, who are 2.5 times more likely to be killed by law enforcement than white men. Over the course of their lifetimes, 1 in every 1,000 Black men and boys will be killed by a police officer.

For decades, community-led movements have called for investments in solutions outside policing. And today, as instances of police brutality become more widely reported on in the media and on social media, more and more Americans are now joining the call to reevaluate the role of law enforcement and to shift some police responsibilities to professionals outside the justice system. In late June, a Public Agenda/USA Today/Ipsos poll showed that nearly 95 percent of Americans thought that policing practices needed to change, with more than half of respondents calling for "major changes" or a "complete redesign" of law enforcement. In particular, there is growing agreement that trained civilians—not law enforcement—should be the primary response to low-level issues within the community. The same poll found that 57 percent of Americans support replacing police officers with clinicians or social workers for concerns related to mental health, substance use, domestic disputes, and school discipline.

These attitudes are consistent with the concept of parsimony in the criminal justice sphere, which holds that the state should never impose consequences more severe than necessary to achieve its goals. Put another way, the criminal justice system, including the police, should employ the lightest touch possible. A parallel to parsimony can be found in the evolution of the practice of medicine, which has now come to emphasize holistic and preventative care. Instead of relying on surgical or other invasive interventions that cause long-term scarring and potential side effects, medicine now looks to first prevent illnesses by encouraging a healthy lifestyle and addressing health issues early with noninvasive treatments. Surgery is not removed as an option but reserved for the most significant situations, and care is taken during the procedure to minimize trauma and promote a quick recovery. Policing and the criminal justice system should be likened to a surgical intervention. While they serve a necessary function, their use should be minimized as much as possible in favor of strategies and interventions with fewer adverse side effects.

Even as public sentiment moves in the direction of redefining public safety and investing in more civilian-based efforts, questions remain on how to operationalize and institutionalize these efforts in an effective way. Over the past 18 months, the Center for American Progress, with support from the Joyce Foundation, brought together a group of experts comprising community leaders, researchers, police professionals, advocates, and practitioners to answer those very questions. CAP framed this issue in a previous report, calling for the establishment of: 1) a dedicated civilian office of public safety within the jurisdiction's government structure; 2) a permanent pathway for community members to participate in the development of jurisdiction's public safety agenda and priorities; and 3) a budgetary mechanism that gives residents direct control over investments in community needs.

Building on those recommendations, this report provides a road map for city governments to establish a civilian Office of Neighborhood Safety (ONS) that provides the infrastructure and resources necessary for successful community-based public safety efforts. With the descriptions of the responsibilities of these offices, city governments can assess the types of proven programs to be implemented, how they can be staffed and funded, and the message they send about a community's approach to safety. The goal is to ensure that community-based interventions are durable, sustainable, and elevated as integral elements of public safety practice—not just an experimental alternative to enforcement.

An ONS is an important step toward a future in which arrest and incarceration are no longer the first response to every issue in society—a future guided by communities most harmed by the justice system, who have been denied a seat at the decision-making table for generations. With the infrastructure to support community-driven solutions, local governments can help bring residents' vision for safety and justice into existence.

Investing in Safety Beyond Policing

Americans have traditionally viewed law enforcement as the primary vehicle for creating public safety, a belief reflected in the organizational structure of most city governments. Typically, law enforcement is one of the only government agencies whose mission is explicitly focused on public safety. Law enforcement agencies also tend to be better funded than other municipal departments, accounting for a significant portion of most city-level budgets. As a result, the police are among the few government agencies with the resources and the mandate to respond immediately to issues around the clock. Officers are thus called on to address any and all tasks related to safety. Elected officials tend to reinforce the preeminence of policing by making them the official face of public safety regardless of their effect on crime rates or on communities. When crime rates drop, city leaders hold a press conference commending the police department; when crime rates increase, the police are rarely held publicly accountable, especially when it comes time to make budgetary decisions.

Compared with policing and the criminal justice system, the ONS is a modern development, though the community-based interventions they employ have been successfully implemented and evaluated over the last several decades. The city of Richmond, California, was on the forefront of the movement, establishing its ONS in 2007 as a tool for preventing gun violence and strengthening community safety and well-being. Since Richmond launched its ONS, roughly a dozen other cities have since followed suit. Unlike the police department or other traditional public safety agencies, Richmond's ONS is not part of the criminal justice system. Instead, it is housed within the city government and staffed by civilians with no authority to enforce the law. This structure is deliberate: Richmond's ONS supports interventions that intentionally operate outside or parallel to the criminal justice system in order to maintain credibility with those at highest risk of violence.

Richmond's ONS has had a profound impact on citywide public safety. When the office was established in 2007, Richmond had the highest homicide rate in California. That year, the city recorded 45.9 homicides per 100,000 people—eight times the national average. Ten years later, in 2017, the city's homicide rate had fallen by 80 percent, to nine per 100,000. ONS programming was associated with a 55 percent reduction in gun homicides and hospitalizations and a 43 percent reduction in firearm-related crimes, according to a quantitative evaluation published in the American Journal of Public Health.

Richmond's innovation provides important lessons for cities that are considering how to shrink the scope of policing and invest in community-driven approaches to public safety. Cities should take caution to avoid reinvesting funding into public institutions that have caused harm and engendered distrust in the community or into agencies that are not equipped to take on roles vacated by the police. Effective interventions require "a major reenvisioning and restructuring of how services and assistance are delivered," explains Thomas Abt, a senior fellow at the Council on Criminal Justice. Accordingly, cities should consider creating a new government structure, specifically designed to meet community safety needs and equipped with the financial resources to match its mandate.

The Significance of Establishing an ONS

An ONS gives cities a way to embed community-based safety solutions into the fabric of government, while still maintaining necessary distance between interventions and the justice system. While cities can support community-based interventions without creating an ONS, it sends a valuable message when these interventions are embedded into government practice. The creation of an ONS is a strong public endorsement of community-based safety solutions, which can help shift the popular narrative that envisions law enforcement officers as the sole stewards of public safety. It signals to residents that these interventions are an important part of the official public safety agenda, on par with policing, and challenges the expectation that law enforcement officers are responsible for addressing all social issues by creating another entity explicitly charged the task.

More than just a tool for accelerating culture change, an ONS provides the foundation for interventions to achieve a meaningful impact on public safety. This can be particularly important when it comes to interrupting chronic violence. Chronic violence is an entrenched problem that will not be solved overnight; violence interventions need stable financial resources and steady political support over a period of several years, and they need adequate time to take hold before their impact is assessed. City leaders should not hastily withdraw funding or support for violence interventions before these interventions have had a chance to realize their full potential.

An ONS can help ensure that community-based interventions receive the sustained support necessary to achieve meaningful, long-term reductions in both violence and the footprint of policing. For one, ONSs can help protect interventions from political instability. Interventions that receive support from political leaders without any formal codification into the government may be vulnerable to elimination in the event of political turnover. Creating an ONS can also insulate against lapses in funding, another common threat to the sustainability of community-based interventions. Whereas interventions have often had to rely on short-term grants, city departments receive funding through the municipal budget to support operations. Annual budget allocations can ensure that an ONS is able to sustain community-based interventions in the long term, even if external funding streams lapse.

[...]

Viewpoint 5

> *"There are many ways to address police misconduct and brutality and improve our law-enforcement system that fit comfortably within a conservative framework."*

Here's What Conservative Law-Enforcement Reforms Should Look Like

Dan Mclaughlin

In the following viewpoint Dan Mclaughlin suggests that some of the reform concepts promoted by the "Defund the Police" movement are compatible with traditional notions of political conservatism, despite opposition from American conservatives. He also examines the issues surrounding law enforcement through the lens of conservative ideals including small government, individual responsibility, and States' rights. His perspective provides an interesting counterpoint to the simplistic "support vs. oppose" debate that often dominates media coverage of the "Defund the Police" movement. Dan Mclaughlin is a Senior Writer at National Review and a Fellow at the National Review Institute.

"What Conservative Law-Enforcement Reforms Should Look Like," by Dan Mclaughlin, National Review, June 11, 2020. Reprinted by permission.

As you read, consider the following questions:

1. The author suggests that conservatives do not believe in the perfectability of humankind. How does he connect this idea to the debates over police reform?
2. Are there any differences between what the author describes as "conservatism" and the type of conservatism exemplified by the contemporary Republican Party?
3. Why does the author suggest that police reform is a quintessential local issue?

In the aftermath of the killing of George Floyd by Minneapolis police officers, the national conversation is focused on how police treat African Americans. As often happens, the loudest voices are left-wing radicals with impractical slogans and an anti-police axe to grind. But that doesn't mean conservatives should be shut out of the policy debate. In fact, there are many ways to address police misconduct and brutality and improve our law-enforcement system that fit comfortably within a conservative framework. At the same time, it falls to conservatives to be careful that reforms do not do more harm than good.

What would conservative law-enforcement reforms look like? Here are the foundational principles from which specific proposals should proceed:

1. Respect for Human Life

Death is an unavoidable part of police work, especially in confrontations with armed civilians where the alternative to a killing by the police is often a killing of the police. As discussed below, the number of unarmed African Americans killed by the police in any given year is quite small, and proportion matters in deciding what changes to make and what tradeoffs to accept. But fundamentally, the first principle of policing must be respect for human life.

That means not treating the relatively small statistical size of the problem as a reason to do nothing at all. It means having respect for the lives of those who interact with the police, respect for the lives of those who depend on police protection, and respect for the lives of the police themselves. "Black Lives Matter" has gained currency as a slogan due to a widespread sentiment among black Americans that their lives are not valued equally. There is no single policy reform that can change that overnight, but conservative leaders should recognize that a consistent pro-life ethic and message stand the best chance of acknowledging the historical roots of the mistrust between cops and African Americans, and of making "Black Lives Matter," "Blue Lives Matter," and "All Lives Matter" into complementary rather than conflicting sentiments. To respect the lives of all, you must respect the lives of each.

2. Personal Responsibility

The core of conservative thinking about misconduct of any kind, in any line of work, is that individuals are responsible for their own actions. Broad-brush generalizations about "all cops" are just as counterproductive and dangerous as generalizations about "all black people." When individuals misbehave, abuse their power, or prey on other people, they themselves should bear the lion's share of the blame and accountability. Conservatives do not believe in the perfectability of mankind: There will always be bad cops, for the same reason that there will always be a need for cops. Moreover, cops exercise government power, which is always prone to abuse and always demands accountability.

The first big step toward individual accountability is to break the power of police unions over the investigation and discipline of individual officers. Conservatives have long argued that unions in general tend to hamstring employers in distinguishing between good and bad employees, and ultimately lead to collective rather than individual responsibility. Public-employee unions in particular are longstanding targets of conservative criticism for undermining democratic accountability in favor of government by the government, of the government, for the government. That is just as true of Republican-aligned police unions as it is of, say, Democrat-aligned teachers' unions.

Whether or not police reform requires breaking the unions themselves or their political influence, states should change their laws going forward to exclude criminal investigations and the officer-disciplinary process entirely from collective bargaining. Calvin Coolidge famously told striking Boston cops that there was "no right to strike against the public safety by anybody, anywhere, any time." No union should have a right to prevent the firing of bad cops in the name of the public safety, either. With unions excluded from bargaining over discipline, there would be fewer obstacles to improving, say, transparency about individual officers' records.

Another way to encourage individual responsibility is to reform qualified immunity, the doctrine that protects police officers from civil suits when they violate individual rights. The doctrine sometimes lets cops off the hook if a right was not "clearly established" in the law. That rule originated with a case where cops got sued for enforcing a statute that the courts later struck down, and in that context, it's appropriate: Cops don't write the laws, and they should not be individually responsible for enforcing a law that a court might later find unconstitutional. But the "clearly established" defense has expanded into situations that solely concern police behavior.

Individual responsibility can also be promoted by preventing police officers from covering their badges, and by regular use of body, dashboard, and interrogation cameras. There are some downsides here: Pervasive use of body cameras, for example, increases the surveillance state in general, because wherever there are cops, there are cameras. And police departments should not be saddled with unreasonable policies regarding retention of vast quantities of video for indefinite periods of time. But promoting transparency in every police department is a further step toward separating bad cops from good ones.

3. Proportion and Deliberation

As the Washington Post has noted, while about 1,000 people are shot to death by the police each year, “The overwhelming majority of people killed are armed. Nearly half of all people fatally shot by police are white. Most of these shootings draw little or no attention beyond a news story.” The Post’s own data show that only nine unarmed African Americans were shot and killed by police last year, and the “number of black and unarmed people fatally shot by police has declined since 2015” at a rate faster than the decline among other groups. Heather Mac Donald elaborates, using the Post data:

> The police fatally shot nine unarmed blacks and 19 unarmed whites in 2019 . . . down from 38 and 32, respectively, in 2015. . . . In 2018 there were 7,407 black homicide victims. Assuming a comparable number of victims last year, those nine unarmed black victims of police shootings represent 0.1% of all African-Americans killed in 2019. By contrast, a police officer is 18½ times more likely to be killed by a black male than an unarmed black male is to be killed by a police officer.

Shootings are not the only source of death, as the George Floyd case illustrates, but this gives a sense of the scale of the problem, and that is always relevant in crafting solutions. Again, the relatively small number does not mean that people who value human life should conclude there is no problem. But it does suggest that radically altering law-enforcement practices could easily lead to more deaths than it prevents. Seventeen people were killed just this past Sunday in Chicago alone. Withdrawing police protection from our cities bears a very real cost in black lives, too, a cost that far too many progressives are willing to ignore.

For all the hullabaloo about “Defund the Police,” American policing has actually grown more slowly than the population: between 1997 and 2016, the number of full-time law-enforcement officers in the United States increased by 8 percent, while the U.S. population increased by 21 percent. A good deal of experience and data show that regular, visible neighborhood beat cops can improve trust, and clustering of police in high-violence hotspots can meaningfully reduce murders. Hamstringing the ability of police departments to use these kinds of proven tactics is simply sacrificing human lives to score political points.

4. Small Government

Small government has never meant "no government." Conservatives have long argued that governments that try to do too many things end up doing more of them badly. That should apply to policing as well. The core of criminal law is predatory behavior: murder, rape, robbery, fraud, arson, vandalism. The further we get from those things, the less we should involve the cops. Historically, the laws that have been most easily abused in racially disparate ways are vague, low-level crimes: loitering, jaywalking, disturbance of the peace. On the other hand, a great deal of disturbance of public order comes from the homeless population, many of whom are mentally ill and should be locked up not as criminals but for their own protection. Reducing criminalization of some of these offenses is more workable if cities are not teeming with disturbed street-dwellers.

Policing should also focus on protection, not raising revenue for the government. The broad use of civil-asset forfeitures that were meant to be confined to major criminal cases, busting people for selling single cigarettes, and other forms of "revenue policing" would all have been recognized by the Founding Fathers as excessive uses of government power.

Then there's drugs. Rolling back the laws on hard drugs would be a mistake, but it's reasonable to rethink the amount of money, time, and manpower that police departments devote to low-level drug crime. And at a minimum, Congress should give states more leeway to experiment with decriminalizing marijuana, given the thorny conflicts that have developed between state and federal laws on the issue.

Proposals to "demilitarize" the police should be on the table, but they should be carefully designed: There is a big difference between police departments' having military vehicles and cops wearing riot helmets. Riot gear is, after all, designed to discourage police officers from seeing their guns as the only line of defense against death or severe injury from thrown bricks and bottles.

5. Federalism and Democratic Accountability

Law enforcement is the quintessential local issue, one that affects people and communities directly. There are more than 15,000 police departments in the United States, and the conditions and communities in which they operate vary widely. The federal government can use its economies of scale to study the matter—e.g. by collecting national data on police violence and misconduct—and promote best practices. But one-size-fits-all solutions are apt to misfire and cause more trouble than they solve. Perhaps just as importantly, it's much easier to get legislation passed in state capitals than it is in today's Congress.

States have a role to play in supervising local authority. The most obvious ways to do this are to put state attorneys general in charge of police investigations in the first instance—thus removing the inherent conflict of interest that arises when local prosecutors are asked to investigate local cops—and to enact statewide legislation on officer discipline.

Federalism and democratic accountability are connected: When police report to an elected official such as a mayor or sheriff, the voters know who to hold accountable for their behavior, whether that means police overreach or police failure to protect citizens. Democratic proposals to expand the Justice Department's oversight of local departments are a step in the wrong direction, leaving local voters nobody to complain to who can be held to account at the ballot box.

States can also step in to provide remedies more tailored to specific problems where federal law is an awkward fit. The qualified-immunity debate, for example, has an unreal quality because the Constitution was not actually written as a manual to micromanage local police officers. Federal courts have repeatedly expanded what qualifies as a "constitutional right" against the police, and then turned around and let cops off the hook by admitting that the courts were making the law up in unpredictable ways. Civil or criminal liability for cops, like civil or criminal liability for any citizen, should in the first instance be governed by clear, written rules made by state legislatures, not by common law fashioned by federal courts.

In the words of Edmund Burke, "a state without the means of some change is without the means of its conservation. Without such means it might even risk the loss of that part of the constitution which it wished the most religiously to preserve." In that spirit, we should welcome debate about how laws are enforced in America. We have made a lot of progress by not standing still: Violent-crime rates have been greatly reduced in much of the country over the past three decades, for example. Conservatives should wish to preserve those gains in crime-fighting and public safety. Improving accountability for law enforcement is part of how we can do that while promoting respect for limited government and the rule of written law. It's also the right thing to do.

Periodical and Internet Sources Bibliography

The following articles have been selected to supplement the diverse views presented in this chapter.

Scottie Andrew, "There's a growing call to defund the police. Here's what it means," CNN, June 17, 2020. https://www.cnn.com/2020/06/06/us/what-is-defund-police-trnd/index.html

Aaron Blake, "The electoral demise of 'defund the police,'" The Washington Post, November 5, 2021. https://www.washingtonpost.com/politics/2021/11/05/electoral-demise-defund-police/

Chris Cillizza, "Even democrats are now admitting 'Defund the Police' was a massive mistake," CNN, November 5, 2021. https://www.cnn.com/2021/11/05/politics/defund-the-police-democrats/index.html

Jessica M. Eaglin, "To 'Defund' the Police," Stanford Law Review Online, June, 2021. https://review.law.stanford.edu/wp-content/uploads/sites/3/2021/06/73-Stan.-L.-Rev.-Online-120-Eaglin.pdf

Steve Friess, "'Defund the Police' Is Dead but Other Reform Efforts Thrive in U.S. Cities," Newsweek, May 24, 2022. https://www.newsweek.com/2022/06/24/defund-police-dead-other-reform-efforts-thrive-us-cities-1709393.html

J. David Goodman, "A Year After 'Defund,' Police Departments Get Their Money Back," The New York Times, October 10, 2021. https://www.nytimes.com/2021/10/10/us/dallas-police-defund.html

Nate Hochman, "Why Are We Still Talking about Defunding the Police?" National Review, October 7, 2021. https://www.nationalreview.com/2021/10/why-are-we-still-talking-about-defunding-the-police/

Zaid Jilani, "The Deadly Consequences of 'Defund the Police,'" National Review, February 1, 2021. https://www.nationalreview.com/2021/02/the-deadly-consequences-of-defund-the-police/

Annie Lowrey, "Defund the Police: America needs to rethink its priorities for the whole criminal-justice system," The Atlantic, June 5, 2020. https://www.theatlantic.com/ideas/archive/2020/06/defund-police/612682/

Anthony O'Rourke; Rick, Su; Guyora, Binder, "Disbanding Police Agencies," Columbia Law Review, Vol. 121. https://www.columbialawreview.org/content/disbanding-police-agencies/

Ari Schulman, "What do 'Defund the Police' and 'Abolish the Police' Really Mean?," The Bulwark, June 10, 2020. https://www.thebulwark.com/what-do-defund-the-police-and-abolish-the-police-really-mean/

Derek Thompson, "Unbundle the Police: American policing is a gnarl of overlapping services that should be demilitarized and disentangled," The Atlantic, June 11, 2020.https://www.theatlantic.com/ideas/archive/2020/06/unbundle-police/612913/

For Further Discussion

Chapter 1

1. What are some of the challenges and complexities associated with studying statistics on police violence?
2. How do historical protests and reform movements focused on law enforcement (e.g. the Newark demonstrations in the late '60s, the riots in L.A. following the Rodney King verdict) compare to contemporary movements like Black Lives Matter and Defund the Police?
3. What are some of the qualities and characteristics associated with the "warrior mentality" that some observers of American law enforcement describe?

Chapter 2

1. What are some of the historical connections between law enforcement and racism or white supremacist groups in American society?
2. Are there demographic categories other than race that are important to include in the analysis of law enforcement violence?
3. What are some of the reasons why it has been difficult to reduce racial profiling by law enforcement officers through administrative and policy changes?

Chapter 3

1. What are some of the potential constitutional issues associated with qualified immunity?
2. What are some of the ways in which court rulings have expanded the scope of qualified immunity in American law?
3. How has the "clearly established law" benchmark shaped the case law associated with qualified immunity for law enforcement?

Chapter 4

1. Is there a difference between defunding and abolishing the police?
2. What can we learn from the results of Camden, New Jersey, disbanding its police force in 2013?
3. Why do some analysts believe that alternative models of public safety like ONS concept could ultimately be more effective than traditional policing?

Organizations to Contact

The editors have compiled the following list of organizations concerned with the issues debated in this book. The descriptions are derived from materials provided by the organizations. All have publications or information available for interested readers. The list was compiled on the date of publication of the present volume; the information provided here may change. Be aware that many organizations take several weeks or longer to respond to inquiries, so allow as much time as possible.

The American Civil Liberties Union (ACLU)

125 Broad Street, 18th Floor
New York NY 10004
(212) 549-2500
website:www.aclu.org

For nearly 100 years, the ACLU has been our nation's guardian of liberty, working in courts, legislatures, and communities to defend and preserve the individual rights and liberties that the Constitution and the laws of the United States guarantee everyone in this country.

Bill of Rights Institute

1310 North Courthouse Rd. #620
Arlington, VA 22201 (703) 894-1776
email: info@billofrightsinstitute.org
website: www.billofrightsinstitute.org/

Established in September 1999, the Bill of Rights Institute is a 501(c)(3) nonprofit educational organization that works to engage, educate, and empower individuals with a passion for the freedom and opportunity that exist in a free society. The Institute develops educational resources and programs for a network of more than 50,000 educators and 70,000 students nationwide.

Campaign Zero

email: feedback@campaignzero.org
website: www.campaignzero.org

Campaign Zero is a social justice project operating under the umbrella of the 501(c)(3) organization WeTheProtesters. Campaign Zero publishes research on police violence and policing practices across the country, provides legal and other assistance to organizers leading grassroots campaigns for police reform, and contributes to the development of model legislation and policy initiatives.

Constitutional Rights Foundation (CRF)

601 S. Kingsley Drive.
Los Angeles, CA 90005
(213) 487-5590
website: www.crf-usa.org

CRF is a nonprofit, nonpartisan, community-based organization dedicated to educating America's young people about the importance of civic participation in a democratic society. Under the guidance of a board of directors chosen from the worlds of law, business, government, education, the media, and the community, CRF develops, produces, and distributes programs and materials to teachers, students, and public-minded citizens all across the nation.

Convergence Center for Policy Resolution

1133 19th Street, N.W. Suite 410
Washington, D.C. 20036 (202) 830-2310
email: info@convergencepolicy.org
website: www.convergencepolicy.org

Convergence Center for Policy Resolution is a 501(c)(3) nonprofit organization focused on solving social challenges through collaboration. The Convergence team brings deep knowledge of policy and process and works with leaders and doers to move past divergent views to identify workable solutions to seemingly intractable issues.

The Institute for Criminal Justice Training Reform

15514 South Western Avenue, Suite D
Gardena, CA 90249
(213) 798-4199
email: info@trainingreform.org
website: www.trainingreform.org

The Institute for Criminal Justice Training Reform is a 501(c)(3) nonprofit organization dedicated to reforming police training procedures around the country to reduce violence and promote public safety. The Institute publishes research and engages in a variety of advocacy efforts related to police reform in the United States.

National Association for the Advancement of Colored People (NAACP)

4805 Mt. Hope Drive
Baltimore MD 21215
(410) 580-5777
email: communications@naacpnet.org
website: www.naacp.org

The National Association for the Advancement of Colored People (NAACP) is a 501(c)(4) nonprofit organization focused on promoting and defending the civil rights and fighting against racism in America. Founded in 1909 by a group including W. E. B. Du Bois, Mary White Ovington, Moorfield Storey, and Ida B. Wells, the NAACP has been at the forefront of civil rights movements in America for over 100 years.

National Police Accountability Project

2022 St. Bernard Ave. Suite 310
New Orleans, LA 70116
email: info.npap@nlg.org
website: www.nlg-npap.org

The National Police Accountability Project (NPAP) is a project operating under the umbrella of the National Lawyers Guild (NLG), a nonprofit membership organization for lawyers, law students, and legal services workers. NPAP is dedicated to reforming law enforcement procedures around the country and eliminating abuse of authority by police and detention officers

United States Courts

One Columbus Circle, NE
Washington, DC 20544
(202) 502-2600
website: www.uscourts.gov

The United States Federal Courts were established under Article III of the Constitution to administer justice within the jurisdiction established by the Constitution and Congress. Federal courts hear cases involving the constitutionality of a law, cases involving a dispute between states, and bankruptcy cases.

Supreme Court of the United States

1 First Street, NE
Washington, DC 20543
(202) 479-3000
website: www.supremecourt.gov

The United States Supreme Court is the highest venue in the nation for legal cases, appeals, and controversies. As final arbiter of the law, the court is responsible for protecting the American promise of justice under the law. The court consists of a chief justice and eight associate justices, who are nominated by the president of the United States with the consent of the Senate.

Bibliography of Books

Radley Balko. *Rise of the Warrior Cop: The Militarization of America's Police Forces.* New York, NY: PublicAffairs, Hachette Book Group, 2021.

Erwin Chemerinsky. *Presumed Guilty: How the Supreme Court Empowered the Police and Subverted Civil Rights.* New York, NY: Liveright Publishing Corporation, W.W. Norton & Company, 2021.

Ben Cohen and Killer Mike. *Above the Law: How 'Qualified Immunity' Protects Violent Police.* New York, NY: OR Books, 2021.

Ross Deuchar, Vaughn J. Crichlow, and Seth W. Fallik. *Police-Community Relations in Times of Crisis: Decay and Reform in the Post-Ferguson Era.* Bristol, UK: Bristol University Press, 2021.

Charles R. Epp, Steven Maynard-Moody, and Donald Haider-Markel. *Pulled Over: How Police Stops Define Race and Citizenship.* Chicago, IL: The University of Chicago Press, 2014.

Anne Gray Fischer. *The Streets Belong to Us: Sex, Race, and Police Power from Segregation to Gentrification.* Chapel Hill, NC: The University of North Carolina Press, 2022.

Matthew Horace and Ron Harris. *The Black and the Blue: A Cop Reveals the Crimes, Racism, and Injustice in America's Law Enforcement.* New York, NY: Hachette Book Group, 2019.

Charles M. Katz and Edward R. Maguire. *Transforming the Police: Thirteen Key Reforms.* Long Grove, IL: Waveland Press, Inc. 2020.

Loretta P. Prater. *Excessive Use of Force.* London, UK: The Rowman & Littlefield Publishing Group, Inc., 2018.

Derecka Purnell. *Becoming Abolitionists: Police, Protests, and the Pursuit of Freedom. New York, NY: Astra Publishing House, 2021.*

Barbara Ransby. *Making All Black Lives Matter: Reimagining Freedom in the 21st Century.* Oakland, CA: University of California Press, 2018.

Katheryn Russell-Brown. *The Color of Crime: Racial Hoaxes, White Crime, Media Messages, Police Violence, and Other Race-Based Harms.* New York, NY: New York University Press, 2021.

Elliott Smith. *Use of Force and the Fight Against Police Brutality.* Minneapolis, MN: Lerner Publications Company, 2022.

Seth W. Stoughton, Jeffrey J. Noble, and Geoffrey P. Alpert. *Evaluating Police Uses of Force.* New York, NY: New York University, 2020. Kim Taylor-Thompson and Anthony C. Thompson. *Progressive Prosecution: Race and Reform in Criminal Justice.* New York, NY: New York University Press, 2020.

Index

E

F

G

H

I

J

K